Mary has been an avid reader since the age of three years. The first thing she had published was in the Newfoundland Magazine of 1984. She decided to start writing seriously when attending a Creative Writing Course and having written several short stories and essays was motivated to try her hand at a full novel. She has also been involved in the production of several technical publications. Mary firmly believes that every cloud has a silver lining, and that age is just a number.

For Toby and Kay.

Mary Grayer Clarke

DARK REGRESSIONS

AUSTIN MACAULEY PUBLISHERS™

LONDON * CAMBRIDGE * NEW YORK * SHARJAH

Copyright © Mary Grayer Clarke 2023

The right of Mary Grayer Clarke to be identified as author of this work has been asserted by the author in accordance with sections 77 and 78 of the Copyright, Designs and Patents Act 1988.

All rights reserved. No part of this publication may be reproduced, stored in a retrieval system, or transmitted in any form or by any means, electronic, mechanical, photocopying, recording, or otherwise, without the prior permission of the publishers.

Any person who commits any unauthorised act in relation to this publication may be liable to criminal prosecution and civil claims for damages.

This is a work of fiction. Names, characters, businesses, places, events, locales, and incidents are either the products of the author's imagination or used in a fictitious manner. Any resemblance to actual persons, living or dead, or actual events is purely coincidental.

A CIP catalogue record for this title is available from the British Library.

ISBN 9781398454460 (Paperback)
ISBN 9781398454477 (Pub e-book)

www.austinmacauley.com

First Published 2023
Austin Macauley Publishers Ltd®
1 Canada Square
Canary Wharf
London
E14 5AA

I owe so much to Austin Macauley Publishers, who have given me this extraordinary opportunity by accepting my debut novel and making me welcome. A special thankyou to Alexander Holiday, Head of Editorial, who showed me kindness and consideration from the start of an exciting journey.

My special thanks go to my son, Toby, and his exceptional wife, Kay, without whom I would not have completed this book let alone found the courage to send it to my very first, publishers.

Finally, thank you to everyone who reads my book.

Author's Forethoughts

Occult – (originally hidden/secret) pertaining to such mystical arts that involve magic, divination, astrology or alchemy. Secret arts considered beyond human understanding – occult arts and sciences.

Occultism – the practice of and belief in occult, necromancy or supernatural powers.

Spiritualism – the belief that spirits of the dead communicate with the living through mediums.

Necromancy – black magic, sorcery, raising of the dead – as the Witch of Endor is said to have raised Solomon.

~

The Occult, it would appear, consists of all the above and has appealed to certain individuals who engaged in such practices since mediaeval times. Probably the best known from the early twentieth century is Aleister Crowley, the author of, *Magick in Theory and Practice*, whose interest stemmed from his undergraduate days at Cambridge. He is reputed to have invoked a curse and stuck a needle in the ankle of a wax model of one of the Tutors. The following day, that Tutor is recorded as having slipped on the steps of the college and broken his ankle.

On another occasion, it is alleged that Crowley and his son MacAleister, his principal proselyte, planned an attempt to raise the god, Pan. They locked themselves in a room, having left strict instructions that no one was to attempt to enter it under any circumstances until the following morning. When the next day his followers opened the door, Crowley was discovered cringing in a corner divested of his robes, apparently incoherent and mentally deranged. For the next several months, he was incarcerated in a lunatic asylum.

MacAleister was dead.

It was therefore assumed that their attempt had been successful.

In the cold light of day, it makes you wonder, doesn't it?

In the latter part of the nineteenth century, there were many influential people practising the black arts of the occult, especially in Paris and Sicily, where Crowley was to eventually reside near Cefalu. It is said that Black Masses were performed at his home, during which blood sacrifices were offered. However, he was not the only practitioner of the occult. Members of such occultist groups frequently disagreed, such splits generating the formation of other such assemblies.

~

In the notes of the psychiatrist Jung, some of the behavioural studies of certain patients are related to the occult. These writings include, among other items, occult phenomena, spiritualism and soul death.

~

I personally have only the basic Christianity beliefs given to me throughout my childhood but as the early years passed, like most teenagers I cast them aside for some years. I had not even considered such things as spiritualism, having scant beliefs and some derision for such practices. However, I was to learn differently in the 1980s, during the first Christmas of my married state.

We were to have lunch with my husband's parents on Boxing Day, then proceed to his maternal aunt for tea, an occasion that my father-in-law preferred to decline. It was, in fact, the first time that I had met these relatives of my husband on a social basis, so knew little about them.

Aunt Doris proved to be some years older than her sister, my mother-in-law, but was by far the more modern in outlook. She was a plump, curled and painted person with a close resemblance to her Pekinese dogs (or perhaps it should be the other way around). Her bust I perceived, firmly led the way, followed as though to balance the equation, by a prominent posterior.

Uncle Stan was a kindly man, very much under the thumb of his wife and three daughters. He was not small, indeed he stood taller and broader than his wife. Only Pat, the eldest, resembled her father in looks and size, but she was a 'bossy-boots.' No doubt inherited from her mother. I had been told that she was married to a rather feckless individual, having apparently tied the knot to ensure the legitimacy of her baby son. Maybe that was true, for Jake was undoubtedly a handsome man, with blond wavy hair, blue eyes, full lips and a great body. He was also blessed with all the blarney of an Irishman who had kissed the stone and I wondered how on earth Pat had managed to get him to tie himself to her with the vows of a marriage ceremony.

The other two, Jenny and Meg, were both nurses and still lived with their parents. Jenny had her father's dark colouring, with her mother's build and dominant character. The stature would follow as a matter of course as she reached middle age. Meg was different altogether, being small and dainty with fair wavy hair and a quiet manner. In a past era, Meg would have been the professional invalid. It wasn't that she was ill, just something that struck me as appropriate. Could Aunt Doris perhaps have resembled this in her youth?

They were an argumentative, noisy family, and although I was somewhat shy, I was made to feel welcome – except by the two horrid Pekinese.

Anyway, after an excellent tea we moved into the sitting room, where after about half an hour of general chat, Meg said, in her excitable bubbly manner, "Shall we do some table tapping?" Then turning to me. "It's sometimes referred to as spirit rapping. The spirits answer any questions put to them, by rapping on the table or tipping it to one side."

I felt rather dubious, but nevertheless inquisitive to discover the tricks associated with such things. Pat, with her husband and father, immediately decided they would prefer to play cards, and returned to the dining room, leaving the rest of us to explore the spirit phenomena.

So it was, that a round table supported on a single centre leg with three splay-clawed feet, was carried before the fire and set down in the centre of the room. Seeing this table, my instinct said that any movement would be comparatively easy with that design, as it tipped with very little pressure on the edges. The lights were dimmed, and we sat around it, hands exposed on the tabletop, little fingers touching. Meg was to be the medium, for although both Aunt Doris and Jenny were also mediums, Meg was apparently by far the most adept of the three.

My first impression was one of chill, despite the bright fire burning in the grate. This, I told myself was the fact that my hands were in a rather unnatural position and unmoving, which would probably have a detrimental effect on the flow of blood to that part of my anatomy. Nevertheless, I felt a frisson of chill creep down my spine, making the hairs on my neck quiver.

Then Meg said, "Is anybody there?"

This made me giggle nervously – she was calling spirits for heaven's sake, of course, nobody was there. My husband nudged me in a way that told me I was embarrassing him, so I shut up.

Meg repeated the question, and this time there was one loud knock from the table.

"Geronimo?" Meg queried.

I grinned to myself, keeping a wary eye on my other half. Well, I ask you, Geronimo! You'd think she could be a bit more imaginative than that wouldn't you? My mother-in-law whispered that this was Meg's Spirit Guide. *Oh WOW!* Apparently, Geronimo was to guide the spirits or Meg on this trip.

Other questions were asked all requiring answers of yes (one tap) or no (two taps), and all were indeed answered, either in this manner or by a slight tipping of the table, applied in the same manner. There was no cloth on the table, and I dared to glance underneath to ascertain who might be the joker but could see no movement of anyone's knees or feet. I was also keeping a careful eye on the touching hands but could see no sign of any movement. Then what was causing this tapping and/or tipping? There is no doubt that this was the kind of scam my husband would thoroughly encompass.

This procedure continued for some time; then Jenny suggested we try the Ouija board for a change. There was some disagreement about this.

"You know your father doesn't like you using that thing. He said you were to destroy it."

"I know, Mum. He thinks we burnt it. Anyway, Dad's playing cards next door, so he won't know."

So, saying, Jenny duly fetched the board from its hiding place upstairs and arranged it upon the table. I saw that the letters of the alphabet were written in a circle around the perimeter. Meg placed a whisky glass upside-down in the centre.

"Now," she said, "everyone places an index finger on the base of the glass."

Then as before, she proceeded to ask questions. The glass moved from letter to letter, spelling out the replies, which Jenny wrote on a pad until the message could be read. I cannot now recall what those were but can confirm that I could not discern a particular pressure of anyone's finger to assist the movement of the glass. In fact, the six digits from time to time left contact with the glass as it moved swiftly from letter to letter. I made it my business to concentrate on keeping watch for an indication of tricks, which was how I came to miss what the instrument was spelling out.

To my horror, someone said, "Oh, there's one for you, wonder what it is?"

It had spelt out the letters of my name, getting my full attention.

"She is here," said Meg, "what is your message?"

The glass continued, "SHE WILL BE BORN IN APRIL."

At that time, only my husband and I knew I was pregnant. We had told no one. In fact, I refused to believe it anyway, despite all the rather obvious signs. After this, of course, it all came out, but the baby was due at the end of May, not April. (Subsequently, on the fourth of April, my daughter was born – a seven-month birth, confirmed by the hospital, where she was placed in an incubator for one month.)

Then laughingly, someone asked another question which, my head being full of other thoughts I once again missed.

But this time the table tipped in my direction, much further than it had done previously, causing me to stand, tipping my chair backwards gravity taking the Ouija board and glass to the floor. It gradually seemed to get more agitated and pushed towards Jenny, who was sitting opposite me. She got up and moved to one side, whereupon the table rose and majestically sailed across the room to the wall. Finding it could go no further it went instead, in an upward direction. The ceilings in the old house were high and it stayed, apparently attracted to it as if by some electromagnetic force, then after a minute or so, descended gracefully to the ground.

~

Although I am aware of the sleight of hand and mind, as practised by such people as Houdini, Uri Geller and David Blane, for whom I have enormous respect as illusionists, I now know full well through personal experience that there are powers out there, beyond our understanding. I saw it with my own eyes and heard it with my own ears. Fact on this occasion was stranger than fiction. The above incident really did happen, but it scared me too, and I swore never again to indulge in anything of this description.

However, whether I approve of it, I am now a firm believer in otherworldly beings. So it is that taking great care not to become influenced by the paranormal,

I have chosen to write about the following strange happenings, the reality of which is for you, the reader, to conclude…

The End and The Beginning

The End and The Beginning

Michael Deville cursed as he lay on his bed of pain.

He had once been a handsome man, with broad shoulders and legs like tree-trunks. In the communal showers, after a game of rugby, the guys referred to him as, *kangaroo balls*. There was no doubt that with his six-foot height, head of thick hair and film star good looks, he could pull any girl he wanted. Now here he was with the choice of either the use of his sharp intellect that had always prevailed or to be free of pain but drugged to a state of near senility. Trouble was, with his brain functioning the pain was almost unbearable.

When he thought back, the disease had probably been creeping up on him over the last ten years, but he'd ignored the twinges and was merely annoyed by psoriasis, which he treated with a proprietary cream.

Nothing could hurt him.

But now here he was at fifty-five. The disease had suddenly flared up and his wife, just a couple of years ago, had finally persuaded him to see a doctor. This visit brought about a referral to see a specialist who diagnosed psoriatic arthritis. This was apparently a more severe type of arthritis, like the rheumatic variety but incorporating psoriasis that would attack his body from within as well as outwardly.

He was obliged to take medical retirement. For a while, he had still been able to drive but the pain soon made this impossible. His joints swelled, but the medication brought him up in blisters. It was changed and they went down again. Then pain flared up. More medication – these worked. He felt better and stopped taking the tablets. He was pain-free and nearly back to normal for a whole five days – then it was back again with a vengeance. The disease developed at an incredible rate of knots and only six months later, he was obliged to take to a wheelchair. Now, just two years later, he was practically bedridden.

He needed a permanent nurse!

He had a permanent nurse!

He was married to a bloody nurse!

"Damn it! Damn her to hell!"

"Oh God, what have I done?"

Michael had heard it said that when struck by nearing death, your life flashes before your eyes. He knew he was indeed marked by death but thought he had time. No quick release for him. It could be six months, six weeks or if he were lucky, six days.

He shouted.

"Helena Rose, bring me my digital recorder. Come on woman, hurry!"

Her real name was Valerie, but Michael had not liked it, so in his arrogance, he had insisted she change it by deed poll.

His nurse/wife quietly entered the room, a small recorder in hand. She was nearly as tall as Michael, fifteen years younger than his first wife who had been ten years younger than himself. Helena Rose was the antithesis of Suzanne, whom he now realised that although older, was nevertheless still small, rounded and pretty. Helena Rose was not by any means unattractive, with her short blond hair and outsized breasts. These were what had first attracted Michael to her. Suzanne had only small hillocks and tiny soft nipples. Those of Helena Rose were a double D-cup, her nipples large and erect.

She had legs that seemed to go on forever, her shoulders broad and square. Whereas little Suzanne had a plump soft posterior, his second wife had an almost masculine bottom.

What have I done? I hate this woman and she hates me.

"Give it here then. Well, what are you waiting for, have you got nothing to do? Get out."

"Can you manage the recorder, Mike?" Helena Rose asked quietly as she retreated to the door.

He hated the abbreviation of his name; it was a privilege only accorded to Suzanne. He didn't allow such shortening of any name, and she knew it. If looks could indeed kill, he would have relieved himself of her irritating presence right then as she left the room but Michael knew he could not manage without her.

Depressing the small button to record was difficult, his fingers had no strength and the pain that shot through them was excruciating. He tried again, swore and exasperated tried to relax against his pillows, squeezing his eyes tightly shut. Unexpected tears rolled down his sunken cheeks, resting in the creases until they dried into crusted, sun-baked rivulets. He would try again later.

"Damn it! I must do it now."

Time was running out, he felt it very strongly. He heard the door slam as Helena Rose left for work. She hadn't even called out goodbye. Michael knew this was the last chance to complete what he had started six months ago.

He must get the rest of his strange story down. Had to try and get the box of notes, recorded discs and memory sticks to Suzanne. He had prepared this box in the beginning, when he could still manage to strike his computer keys but that was no longer an option.

How much longer had he before…?

~

It had all started when, prior to his retirement and while he still had the ability to move around, if only slowly and painfully. He decided it was time to sort through the boxroom where old photographs and papers were stored. Many hours were spent with only nostalgia for company, whilst he looked at photographs, letters, old birthday cards and school reports. Year's old electricity and tax bills were duly shredded along with the love letters and cards from Suzanne. He found an old box that had contained five reams of A4 printer paper and placed the photos therein – they would be passed to his first wife.

That was when after gazing into a space occupied only by his memories and dreams, Michael shook himself and continued the task he had set himself. Which was when he discovered a box containing things of which he had no memory whatsoever. There was an old-fashioned reel-to-reel tape, books of notes, apparently made by a psychiatrist by the name of Dr Jennings and two obviously very old handwritten diaries. These finds he put to one side to investigate the contents sometime in the future and basically forgot about it until…

~

The dreams had started on the 4th of August 2016. He remembered the date exactly because it was his birthday. They occurred only when he was alone in the house and was completely relaxed either dozing on the recliner or on his bed.

In the beginning, he had thought the dreams to be simply that, dreams – based on childhood memories – but there were anomalies.

On waking the memory of these dreams was still clear in his head, so intrigued, he decided to record them, complete with comments. This he commenced to do daily, typing his memories into the computer that sat on the desk in the corner and saving them onto a memory stick. This machine was not connected to the Internet, Helena Rose had her own laptop on which Michael assumed she joined chat groups. She paid for the broadband connection out of her own earnings so he couldn't care less. Apart from anything else, that fact meant she would not attempt to use his PC, thereby giving him privacy.

Time passed and the dreams increased profoundly. So it was that over the past eighteen months Michael recorded each occurrence. As his strength deteriorated, he began to record the details onto his newly acquired digital recorder, carefully transferring them to his computer on a regular basis.

The dreams! No! He would not think about it.

~

That was when he remembered the box that he had now stashed under his bed and decided it was time to explore the contents. The notes he was soon to discover seemed to apply to him and for some unknown reason, he appeared to be unable to read the two diaries. They were obviously written in English, and he assumed from the script that women were the owners of these books but the words just blurred whenever he tried to read them. A magnifying glass made not one jot of difference, so Michael put them to one side and made a phone call to an old acquaintance with an interest in recording devices. Joe, it seemed would be only too happy to sort out the required device for reel-to-reel transcription and would deliver the same the next day – price negotiable in cash. The deal duly done, Michael prevailed upon Joe to thread the tape ready to play, foreseeing many struggles and rather blue air in the future. Then he set the equipment together with the box to one side until he felt inclined to deal with it.

Things had changed as time progressed and now, he had only to relax, think of his strange dream world and he was in regression, living as though at that point in time. It scared him, but the thing that frightened Michael most was that the dreams, visions, regressions or whatever they were, always included him but left his body behind. What if he couldn't get back into himself? *Perhaps that wouldn't matter though, for in a different time warp he was free from his incapacity and pain.* That character, although living in a different time, he could still recognise as his own essence.

When it started, he was intrigued. *The episodes*, as he now referred to them in his mind, had about them the feeling of reality, memories being replayed in the form of dreams or visions. But that wasn't quite right; it was perhaps more like a form of remote viewing in regressive format. He had always felt he had the ability to read the minds of others but acknowledged to himself that this might be more the power to control other people, using that aptitude to steer them in the direction he required.

Michael wasn't quite sure why he had done so but when he awoke from the first experience, he diligently typed the details on his computer, saved it to a memory stick and placed it carefully to one side. Then on the lid of the box containing the reel-to-reel tapes etc., he sellotaped an envelope clearly addressed to Suzanne and marked, *PRIVATE*. A letter within, written in scrawling print the pen held awkwardly between misshapen painful fingers, read…

SUZANNE, MY DARLING SUZANNE – PLEASE DON'T GIVE UP ON ME. PLEASE READ WHAT IS WRITTEN ON THE MEMORY STICKS AND THEN PLAY THE FINAL RECORDINGS. THE REEL-TO-REEL TAPE WILL ADD SOME PROVENANCE TO MY RAMBLINGS. THERE ARE ALSO TWO DIARIES THAT APPEAR TO BE WRITTEN IN ENGLISH BUT WHICH I AM TOTALLY UNABLE TO DECIPHER, PERHAPS YOU WILL HAVE MORE LUCK. WHAT YOU CHOOSE TO DO WITH THEM AFTERWARDS IS YOUR DECISION, BUT I'M NOT MAD. WELL, I JUST MAY BE, BUT THE STORIES, MY REGRESSIONS, ARE TRUE, I SWEAR. ARE MY EXPERIENCES PROOF THAT THESE PEOPLE WERE ME IN PREVIOUS LIVES? OF COURSE, THE FIRST BIT SEEMS TO HAVE BEEN ME IN MY EARLY LIFE. DID I SEE A DR JENNINGS THE PSYCHIATRIST, DID I DO WHAT HE REVEALS AND HAVE FORGOTTEN? HOWEVER, THE DETAILS SEEM TO COVER A PERIOD A FEW YEARS PRIOR TO MY ACTUAL BIRTH IN 1963.

I AM SO SORRY SUZANNE, FOR ALL THE PAIN, I HAVE CAUSED YOU. I SHOULD HAVE SAID IT MUCH SOONER – I LOVE YOU SUZANNE – ONLY YOU.

YOUR MIKE….XX

That was when he realised that the ability to type and write was fast abandoning him. The box now contained several memory sticks each carefully numbered, some pages with his notes and comments, also numbered and placed in their appropriate sequential position between the sticks, plus Michael's digital recorder. It must be done now.

~

It took another three hours before he had finished.

Michael sighed, relaxed for ten minutes, knowing he must put the items in the box and make sure he properly secured it with sticky tape. This was not easy, for today every pressure on his curled-under toes was agony, shooting pain through his feet and legs into his groin.

"I will do it. I must."

Michael gritted his teeth, but that hurt too. He was not expected to get out of bed whilst alone nowadays, a urine carafe having been left by the bedside for his convenience, so the wheelchair was at the end of the bed. He wriggled and slid along the mattress until he could reach it, then with a burst of determination, Michael slid himself into the wheelchair. Breathless, he sat for some minutes then pushed the lever to drive, with difficulty, released the brake and guided himself to his filing cabinet.

"Damn!" he swore, remembering that it was locked. This was where all his private papers were kept, the key always hung around his neck on a strong leather thong. It is not easy to remove a thong from around one's neck when your arms are locked shoulder to elbows and your backbone is fused at the neck, making it painful and somewhat difficult to move. It took seven attempts before he could finally dislodge it, nearly dropping the key as he inserted it into the lock. However, he had remembered to loop the thong around his wrist before attempting to open the cabinet, having been caught out that way once before. Finally, the lock turned, and Michael pulled drawer three (the one most conveniently within his reach) of four open. From it, he levered the box it contained onto his lap. Spinning the chair, he returned to the bed to retrieve the recorder, awkwardly inserting it into its place. Then he replaced the lid, firmly taping it in position and sticking a self-adhesive label along each side, in such a way that should the box be opened, it would be obvious. At the beginning of the project, he had typed on them:

This seal must not be broken before handing it to the addressee.

He turned to replace the box…

This was where Helena Rose found him when she returned at six o'clock that evening. He was clutching the box tightly to him with a look of fear on his face, his mouth open in what could have only been a scream. His eyes were open – darkly ominous – staring at her as she entered the room, but she was once a nurse and knew death when confronted by it. Nevertheless, she closed his eyes and mouth before telephoning Michael's doctor and long-time friend. Richard.

Part 1
Michael Deville 1963–2018

1

Michael's remains were interred in the cemetery of the village church one Wednesday afternoon in April. Suzanne did not want to go, after all, he was no longer related to her. However, Helena Rose telephoned with the news and had begged her to attend. Having ascertained who would be going to the funeral and discovering that it did not include the other woman's daughters, she agreed to attend.

Afterwards, Suzanne went to the old house she had once loved. People with whom he had worked tried to find complimentary things to say about the man who had from time to time made them feel important, only to discover that they had been useful to him in one way or another. They believed he thought of them as his friends and as such, were invited to drop in for drinks and nibbles at Christmas time. Later in the year they felt unable to refuse to repair his boiler, paint the exterior of the house or whatever, all free of payment, except for some great meals provided by Mrs Mike, which was what these acquaintances had once dubbed Suzanne.

All this ceased when the new wife took over – the Boss changed.

Michael would have hated this, Suzanne thought, drinking a glass of wine, silently toasting her ex-husband, then sought out Helena Rose to say goodbye.

"Just a minute, Suze, Mike left a box of stuff for you, in fact, he was clutching it when I found him."

Ah! Suzanne remembered their recent telephone conversations and her visits to the house, something that was unknown to his second wife.

"Here you are."

Helena Rose dumped the box in Suzanne's arms.

"There's his old reel-to-reel tape recorder too – old classical music tapes I suppose. You like that stuff too so you're welcome. Go on then, open it up. Let's see what's in there."

"I don't think this is the time. I'll open it later, at home."

"Oh! But you will let me know what's in there, won't you? After all, Mike was my husband. I've got a right to know."

Suzanne felt a glow of satisfaction.

"I don't think so. After all, it is clearly marked as private. Michael obviously went to a great deal of trouble to seal the box to avoid interference. Anyway, I see no reason for us to ever meet again."

And so, saying, she left the house for the last time, determined to never even pass through that village again, if it was possible to avoid doing so.

2

Suzanne's Notes

I did, of course, have some idea of what to expect in that box, but must confess that I did not expect it to be so well organised. Michael had never been one to be immaculate, except where model railways were concerned. Certainly, he was very adept as regards the organisation of others and quick to note any discrepancy on their part, but where paperwork was concerned there was no interest – so get someone else to sort it out.

I looked through the contents then replaced the lid. I would concentrate on that lot when I had time to spare. For the next month, I was off on an assignment abroad, so as was my usual procedure, all personal papers, such as house documents etc. were deposited in my safe. This time, something made me place Michael's box in there as well. Anyway, that's what I did, and when I returned a month later, it was to find my house had been trashed. Strangely though, nothing appeared to have been taken. *Could someone has been searching for Michael's box?*

I had previously only read the note attached to the box top, glanced through the contents and noted the tapes, memory sticks and recorder discs, plus a few sheets of paper filled with Michael's somewhat illegible scrawl. There were also a couple of what appeared to be rather tatty diaries, written at some time in the distant past by two women, Isabella de Ville and Susan Blessed.

I would have to concentrate to decipher the writing and as I noted each sheet was also numbered, it would presumably be to my advantage to go through it all sequentially. Anyway, Michael's short note made me cry, remembering the good times, and I wasn't ready to deal with that yet.

I phoned the local police station to report the break-in and much to my surprise a couple of constables arrived within the hour. They introduced themselves as PC Thelma Baker and PC Chris Troy.

"Would you like a cup of tea?" I asked. "I've been travelling since 6.30 this morning and I am absolutely whacked."

Both accepted my offer and whilst I waited for the water to boil PC Troy inspected the damage. The female officer stayed with me in the kitchen.

"May I call you Suzanne?" she asked. "Please call me Thelma."

"Yes, of course," I replied. "Do you think you can find three mugs amongst the debris, please? I'd better wash them before they're used."

Thelma not only found the mugs but washed them. I liked her.

Then, sitting around the kitchen table I answered their questions as to my whereabouts, explaining that all my private papers and valuable jewellery had been locked in my safe. I confirmed that having checked the contents I was quite happy that no one had discovered its whereabouts. I did not feel it necessary to supply a list of its contents or whereabouts.

The two police officers had arranged for forensic officers to check the premises. After they had finished dusting for fingerprints and lecturing me on security, I had a much-needed shower and fell into bed where I think I must have slept as soon as my head touched the pillow.

The next morning, I arrived somewhat late at the offices of the magazine for which I did some freelance work and handed my stories to the magazine editor. Then I departed for a welcome two-week break. I had no intention of going away; I did enough travelling as a journalist. For me, a holiday was the ability to remain at home, peacefully doing whatever I wanted. And what I really wanted was to spend time in the garden and do some necessary decorating. I would also read and listen to what Michael had apparently intended for only my attention.

I had known him well. He was a cruel, narcissistic character but nevertheless a very clever man, certainly not given to any form of fantasy, and having spoken to him in those last weeks, I'm sure he was not mentally impaired. On the other hand, it was obvious to me that he no longer trusted Helena Rose (whom I think of as HR) and was certainly frightened of or by something.

~

I spent two whole days sorting out my trashed home, washing and replacing clothes back in cupboards and drawers, then doing the same thing with kitchen crockery and cutlery, having first put everything I could through the dishwasher. I ended up with three black plastic bags of old clothing and broken bits and pieces. It was probably a good thing. I store so much stuff, being reluctant to chuck things away, and fortunately, none of the bits and bobs that I treasured had been broken.

As I spoke to each of my Quarry Critters (a collection of stoneware dogs) in turn by name, I considered the possibility that perhaps it was I who was doolally, not my late ex-husband!

On the third day, the guy who keeps my garden basically tidy was due for his fortnightly visit, so leaving Steve to it I took my bags of rubbish to the tip and charity shop, then went shopping for paint. I spent the afternoon preparing the kitchen walls for painting and was all ready to start the following morning. I worked until the job was finished – that's my way – then cleared up, soaked my aching body in a hot bubble bath, and then went to the local hostelry for a much-needed meal. Well, I didn't feel like cooking, and anyway, the paint might not have been properly dry. It was 12.15 pm before I was finally in bed with a good book, and when I awoke some eight hours later, the book was face down on the bed beside me – open at page two!

Day four was a perfect summer's day, so I settled myself comfortably on the patio beside the pond with my laptop and printer and Michael's box of tricks.

Once again, I read his last letter to me, declaring his love. We seemed to have lost so much that could have been, but I remembered how psychotic he could be. I booted up and inserted the first memory stick…

~

I sit here at my keyboard and with a perfect recall of my dream/vision or whatever. Memories flash through my head as I recall appointments with Doctor Jennings all those years ago. I am not sure exactly what happened, but it was as though I was actually there in the past. It could just be that my recall at having these memories jogged was overly sharp, or more likely as it seems to me, that I was dreaming. Surely it must have been a dream, why otherwise were there some things that I feel sure never really happened? Or did they?

Added later:

(It was only much later, I realised that these strange experiences might be a form of regression, that I am not sleeping and dreaming, but do, in fact, enter a trance state. It is almost like moving in another dimension – another plane. Could it be Astral-Projection, perhaps? No, not that, for I understand from an old friend who was (she's dead now) very into that kind of thing, that projection

is an action controlled by oneself.) Or maybe Time-Travel? Do I enter a memory that can draw me into its mode like entering a computerised virtual world? I like that one and have decided to think of future experiences as entering my Magic Memory Mode (MMM).

Who am I?

Am I mad?

You may well decide that to be the case by the time you finish with this box of 'stuff' but do please, dear Suzanne, give it some consideration and perhaps you may come to a sensible conclusion. If you are reading this, I have obviously left this mortal coil, and if my regressions are truly my past existences, I wonder what state the world will be in when I make my next appearance!

Whatever, Suzanne! These notes are for your eyes only now and I will set the memories/experiences down as they happen, with the intention of adding anything further that might occur. As I'm not quite sure if the person is me or not, I shall write as the narrator of these various items.

3

Item #1

"Mr Jennings would be furious. Michael was late last week."

He broke into a run. Crossing the busy main road was almost impossible, and his appointment with the psychiatrist was at two-thirty. Finally, he managed to get halfway across. Perhaps, I can make it in five minutes, he thought. Sticking up his hand to the squeal of brakes and tooting horns he dashed the rest of the way over the road.

"Oh, Mr Deville, you're on the dot."

There was a sarcastic note in Debra Dennison's voice. Michael was about to make a retort, but she continued speaking.

"He said to tell you to go right in as soon as you arrived."

She waved a hand in the direction of Dr Jennings' door, so with a broad wink he knew would make her blush with pleasure, he knocked and walked straight into the room.

Jennings was a tall, thin man of gangly appearance. He was invariably dressed in a black shirt with blood-red tie and a black suit, the matching leather shoes shining so brightly that they reflected. His hair was also black, smooth against his head from a peak low on his forehead. Shuddering involuntarily, Michael was reminded of Count Dracula, having recently read Bram Stoker's book, realising that what he felt about this man was fear. He didn't like that one bit, preferring to be totally in charge and wondered how such a character came to be such a big name in the field of psychiatry.

"Ah, Michael!"

~

His mellifluous voice flowed over Michael. It's like being wrapped in a soft mohair blanket, and he relaxed into the large soft armchair that was the psychiatrist's preference over the usual couch.

"You have been running, relax and catch your breath. Count slowly…one…two… three…"

He counted to himself and felt his heartbeat slow; his breath became even. He felt safe now.

"You are ten years old, it is night-time, dark. Where are you, Michael?"

The answer came in the voice of a tearful ten-year-old boy.

"I'm in bed. They're going to put me in a children's home for being naughty."

"What did you do?"

"I ambushed Rick Chambers in the cemetery, tied him up and pushed him down a freshly dug grave, then threw leaves on top of him." Whining now – *"It was only a game. Rick's a coward. He screamed and yelled 'til someone found him. I was going to get him out later."*

"But you didn't, Michael, did you? You forgot about him; poor Rick was in that pit for over an hour."

Michael giggled.

"Yeah, I forgot him. I was playing football then it was teatime. Then his dad came around to our house and told on me, and she *yelled at me and said I had to go straight to bed, and they'd think about whether to put me in a home for bad boys."*

He remembered how scared he'd been, how he curled up under the blankets in the dark…thought about it. Then Jennings spoke, bringing him back in line.

"Michael? Tell me what happened then."

"She was going to pour boiling oil in my eyes. I'm scared to go to sleep in case I miss her creeping in."

He appeared to be really scared, shivering with apprehension.

"Who are you afraid of, Michael?"

"Her. My mother! She hates me. She wants me to be blind, so I won't be able to see to do bad things."

"Relax Michael, you are safe now…"

"In the distant future, when you will once again remember your visit to me today, you will automatically regress. Now I shall count backwards and when I reach one, you will wake up. You will feel refreshed and will not remember what we have discussed. Three…two…one."

~

Michael was so comfortable in this armchair. He stretched his arms above his head and asked Dr Jennings in an arrogant voice, "What great insight do you presume to offer me for my problem?"

"I would suggest that you find yourself a good wife who will take care of your needs and with whom you can set up a home of your own. You will then be in control of your own domain, and I suspect life will become more to your liking."

Michael liked that.

"Should I see you again, Dr Jennings?" he asked.

"I think if you take my advice, you will not find that necessary. Meanwhile, here is an exemption form, which you should return to the appropriate National Service office. I have signed it, as I feel you are unsuited to military service."

"Thank you, sir," was the more polite tone of voice.

Picking up the precious piece of paper, Michael shook his hand and left the practice for the last official time, not, of course, forgetting to flirt and banter with the delectable Debra. Not the type of person he deemed to be worthy of him, of course, but he considered it his duty to allow any attractive woman the excitement of his attention.

Safely outside and around the corner out of sight, Michael jumped high, punching the air, having achieved what he wanted, exemption from military service. *What a clever fellow I am, he thought – what an actor.* He had been attending consultations with the psychiatrist for the past six weeks. *Fancy the stupid little man thinking he could hypnotise me!*

In just three weeks he would graduate he was almost a Bachelor of Science. Naturally, he was confident of receiving a first-class honours degree. The trouble had been that his deferment of military service was also at an end, and he would be expected to go into the army for two years. Michael very definitely did not want this, hence his so-called mental problems.

Good, eh! He thought.

But he liked this idea of having a home of his own, with a little wifie to run it and look after yours truly. A life controlled entirely by him. It was time to start perusing the available females to enable him to choose the necessary chattel.

~

Of course, at that time he did not have the notes or tape. He was not aware that Dr Jennings had, in fact, hypnotised him.

~

The next item, carefully inserted in sequence, was a handwritten note from Michael.

As I mentioned earlier, there may be some anomalies in my first Magic Memory Mode experience. However, I find amongst his notes that Jennings did, in fact, issue an exemption certificate. Pity, because it was only a few months later that conscription was withdrawn and had I not had those appointments with that man, perhaps my final years may have been less self-destructive.

I must confess that I had completely forgotten it, but I do now recall seeing a psychiatrist when I was still at university and his name was indeed Jennings. The reason I had an appointment in the first place made through my GP Dr Savage, was that there were times when I sort of blacked out. I just stopped whatever I was doing, once driving my motorbike into a heap of gravel. These episodes lasted for only two or three minutes, if that, but were somewhat disconcerting. Anyway, that was in the early 1980s and we were a firm 'couple' then.

I find myself skipping between acknowledging the psychiatrist as either Dr Jennings or Dracula – not sure why but feel I should mention it here.

~

A caffeine fix was sure to be needed. I remembered that on one occasion before we were married, Michael had skewed the Lambretta off the country road we were traversing on our way to work, into a heap of gravel, narrowly missing a ditch. When I asked what had happened, he told me to just shut my mouth and hang on. Then he drove back onto the road and nothing more was said of the matter. From which he had not recovered from the debility requiring psychiatric treatment. However, I must say that to my knowledge there was no recurrence after we married.

I printed the contents, having decided to save all the information I discovered in the box onto my computer hard disc, complete with any comments and notes I might make in the process, then backed it up onto a thumb-drive. Each page thus printed would be placed face down in a box file, duly labelled, *REGRESSIONS*. In this way, I would have an original hard copy plus what I put on my computer, with backup and Michael's 'box of stuff.' Belt and braces perhaps but my house had been trashed once and I was feeling a bit paranoiac.

The next bit was handwritten so before getting down to deciphering it, I made a mug of coffee.

~

As I settled down for a quiet read, I pondered on my earlier recollection. The next thing I remember is waking with the following clear in my mind. This dratted disease may imprison me, but my recall is as perfect nowadays as it was in my teens and twenties. However, although I clearly remember what happened in Magic Memory Mode, (MMM) I cannot believe I indulged in the breaking and entering Dr Jennings' office. Nevertheless, I apparently acquired the enclosed notes and tape somehow, therefore they can reasonably be assumed to have been illegally procured. However, they are now in your possession, so be careful not to get into trouble through my misdemeanours.

Am I in the past or the present? I am not sure now but surely there will be a clear answer to my questions soon. When you read the next MMM, you will, like me, be unsure of the place in time.

Perhaps you can check out the delectable Debra – did she get a divorce and run off with her paramour I wonder?

I shall not expect you to struggle with my poor script any more than necessary, Suzanne, so will continue my tale on the memory stick.

~

4

I had no intention of entering the office of Dr Jennings ever again but that night as I lay in my bed, mentally celebrating my ingenuity and brilliance, I recalled that he would have notes and maybe even tapes about me. What had he written? Had he made up things from my replies that I had not meant? Did he drug or hypnotise me?

I had read a great deal about psychiatry, prior to my agreement to allow myself to be assigned to one of them and discovered that it was the usual practice for them to record each session. Good old Doc Savage, the GP, who had brought me into the world and was a trusted friend of my mother, had also told me the general procedure so far as he was aware, which confirmed what I had read.

The more I thought about it, the more I knew that something would need to be done. So, I set the Great Brain to work, or as Hercule Poirot would have said, *'The leetle grey cells'* and came up with a couple of ideas.

Subsequently, I dumped the one where I would seduce Debra Dennison, the secretary, when Dr Jennings was out. I would give her a drugged drink, get her into his office, into her knickers and hump her until she fell asleep…but no. Apart from anything else, she was at least thirty-five and too well padded for my taste. I am a straightforward man so I might say something ill-advised. She might repeat the details of my visit to her boss – no, not a good idea. Okay, Plan B is the one to put into effect.

I waited until the following Friday when I knew the office would be closed for the weekend. With my amazing recall, I visualised the secretary's office. There were four doors – one, of course, was the entrance from the foyer, marked Dr Jennings – Reception. Inside in the right-hand wall, was a door providing direct access to Dracula's room. The remaining two were directly facing the entrance door, one being a walk-in stationery cupboard, incidentally, also containing a safe and two filing cabinets. The other was a small windowless kitchen, with a sink, set into a small worktop, on which sat a coffee machine and kettle. There were cupboards under this fixture and more on the left-hand wall, doors and drawers painted an uninteresting cream. These two small rooms were each roughly three by four metres, and I was aware of their contents because I had looked in them during a short absence of Debra during my third visit.

I knew the office would be empty just after 3.30 pm and, having had an hour-long appointment at 2.30 pm for the last six Fridays, I also knew that Debra always spent that time doing her filing for the week, in the stationery room. I was also aware that Dracula always short-changed me, and I was usually out of his consulting room twenty minutes or so short of 3.30. Then first Dracula would leave the premises, followed shortly afterwards by Debra, just in time for her to don her coat and lock up.

So it was that the following Friday I waited for my replacement 2.30 to show up, and just followed her in as she opened the door. She was what I always think of as 'the faded film star' type, probably nearer fifty than forty, and desperately trying to hold on to her looks. Her figure didn't look bad, but her carriage showed that she was pretty well corseted. Mind you, not everyone would have noticed but of course, not everyone is as observant as I am. Anyway, we went in together and I gave her my devastating smile. It got to her, as I knew it would, no woman can resist it when I look at her that way, and she would probably have murdered for a toy boy like me.

I headed towards the stairs that led to the consulting rooms of another psychiatrist, and when she was out of sight, backtracked to a dark corner beneath them, where I stayed for the next hour and twenty-five minutes. Jolly uncomfortable it was too. I might have known that a woman like 'faded film star' would appeal to Jennings – just his type, so there was no way he was going to cut her appointment short. I would like to have been a fly on the wall for that one.

She eventually left, followed within five minutes by Jennings. I knew Debra would be leaving as soon as he was clear. If the boss leaves early, why should his secretary stay until five?

As soon as he exited the building, I dashed to the door marked 'Reception' and pushing it just a little way open, inserted a piece of Wrigglies best in the lock. When Debra left, she released the catch and pulled the door shut behind her, hurried out. I pushed it open, removed the gum and locked myself on the receiving side. *Brilliant, eh!*

I had a momentary glitch when I discovered that the door to Dr Jennings' office was locked. However, a quick search through Debra's desk drawers provided a bunch of keys, one of which fitted the locked door. It also revealed a cache of letters, tucked carefully into a small jiffy-bag. Who would have thought plump old Debra would be carrying on a salacious affair with her brother-in-law? Silly bitch! Fancy keeping written evidence. That is something I would never do. They made interesting reading though and explained her rush to leave as early as possible on Friday afternoons.

Another key from Debra's desk proved to fit Dracula's desk drawers. Upon opening the top centre one I found what I had suspected, a compact tape recorder, still containing the latest, according to the label, for a Ms Gillian Torrance. The name rang a bell – Ben Torrance is a professor at the university – something to do with oceanography. I would have loved to listen to it but someone passing might hear. So, I concentrated on a set of locked drawers against the wall behind the desk. This was easy. The bottom drawer was labelled *PATIENTS – PREVIOUS*. It proved to contain files and I soon found Deville-M. It didn't take long to replace its contents with a similar number of papers from a fat file at the back of the drawer, and I put the papers in a manilla envelope, acquired from Debra's selection of such things. No one was likely to notice that the notes from the Deville file had been replaced.

Unfortunately, I could not find any tapes, other than the one still on Dracula's machine. Perhaps they were in a safe but although I tried the obvious places, behind pictures, wall panels etc., I never found one. So, I decided to try Debra's filing system in the stationery room. Her bunch of keys easily opened the cabinets where low and behold, one of them contained reel-to-reel tapes appertaining to discharged patients. I removed mine, locked it up and returned to reception.

I had allowed myself about ten minutes, but Debra's letters had delayed me, and I realised that twenty minutes had passed. I could have spent all night in there going through files but thought I'd better get out – just in case.

Anyway, I couldn't afford the time, as I had made a date with the person, I thought might be suitable as my future wifie.

~

The next section was added sometime later. I assume he must have realised how confusing his mishmash of information might be for me, and Michael had written in bold type:

'Continues from previous but please consider it as Item 2.'

5

Item #2

Her name was Wendy, and she was a couple of years younger than yours truly. She was still at the Convent and had just taken her exams for university. I had known her since I was fifteen. I always found Convent girls very willing even anxious, for an experience of sex. Probably because of the all-female environment, and a natural desire to rebel against the establishment.

The subversive rebellion was the way I had always reacted at St Pat's, a boy's only school, run by Jesuits. Hell! I wasn't even a Catholic. Anyway, with my photographic memory, I'd never needed to bother much with homework, just half an hour to scribble it down in time for the ritualistic homework hour with Father Franklyn. Which left me with time to spare for the all-important sexual experience. But I digress.

However, Wendy had always proved strong where seduction was concerned. Now I was going to try not only to seduce her but also to dissuade her from going to university where she intended to study law but to marry me instead.

Wearing grey slacks with a cream turtleneck shirt and a blazer, I turned up at the pre-arranged meeting place only twenty minutes late. Another of my little ploys, I find that a girl will hang around for nearly an hour.

I kept one waiting outside the cinema one night and watched her. She walked up and down, periodically peering around the corner just in case she was in the wrong place after all. When only five minutes short of the hour, she gave a final look at her wristwatch and turned to walk away, which was when I called her name. She looked about to bawl me out, so I jumped in quickly. "You're early, it's only five to. Have you been waiting long?" That, of course, immediately cooled the situation as she was no longer sure that we had arranged to meet at six or seven o'clock.

Does that little anecdote ring any bells, Suzanne? Sorry.

Anyway, Wendy was waiting for me, looking just the sort of girl I could comfortably take home to meet my mother. Clothes would be one of the first things I would take in hand. She was wearing expensive, casual dark green shoes, but flat, matching her warm green coat that was crimped in at the waist with a high deep collar, pulled up to protect her from the wind. Later, I saw that she wore a grey skirt that came below her knees and a polo-neck sweater, again in her favourite dark green. She had full breasts and quite good legs. I visualised her in a full shocking-pink skirt with a very low-cut black top, something off the shoulders, possibly trimmed with fur, worn with high black stilettos. Mmm! Just thinking about it turns me on.

I had splashed out for the evening by taking her to a rather nice restaurant. She could have dressed up a bit you'd think. We ordered our food, and I did the impressive bit with the wine tasting. Can't think why – they open a brand-new bottle then give the punters a chance to critique the contents…a load of rubbish in my opinion, but it goes down well with the fillies.

Wendy made one glass of wine last all the evening and wouldn't accept a top-up. I tried to break the ice by talking about university, which was when I came to the full understanding that she was not under any circumstances a suitable wifie for yours truly.

I asked, "Do you really want to go to university for all those years of study? What if you wanted to get married?"

She laughed, as though I'd made a joke.

"If I should, at some time in the future, decide to marry, it will have to fit around my career as a barrister. Getting there is going to take me at least ten years. Anyway, why on earth should I want to be saddled with a man who would probably be under the misapprehension that I was there for his convenience? No way Jose!"

That confirmed my thoughts, and I certainly wasn't going to get lucky tonight. Now I had to fix up another date with another girl – damn it! This could be expensive.

~

Celia was my next choice. She was from the same background as Wendy so far as education was concerned, and the same age. However, all similarities ended there. Celia was a keen sportswoman. She rode a boy's racing bike, with drop handlebars, played tennis for her school and was in the county team. She also swam competitively, was shortlisted for the Olympic relay race team, skated and played ice hockey during the season. Generally, an all-rounder. Oh! I nearly forgot, Celia also rode horseback and indulged in foxhunting (Daddy was Master of the Hunt). He was a straight-backed, boring old fart if ever there was one.

Anyway, Celia was definitely one of the crowd – a good sort – known amongst us chaps as, the *Hunt Bicycle.*

Do you remember when we went to the Hunt Ball, Suzanne, with you in seven layers of pink net over taffeta? It was ballerina length, and you were the Belle of the Ball.

My date with her was to be a trip to the theatre. Personally, I loathe musicals, but I knew through the grapevine that she was mad about them, and something or other big from America, complete with a star cast, was coming to the local Gaumont Theatre. So, I got a friend who was going into town to book and pay for a couple of tickets and then I phoned Celia to finalise the arrangements. The tickets were to be held for Deville at the kiosk, but by the time I arrived, they had already been picked up.

"The gentleman said two seats in the circle had been reserved in the name of Deville, sir. He and the young lady arrived and went straight up about fifteen minutes ago."

That was that. The bitch used the tickets I had paid for and left me standing like a lemon. The only reason I'd arranged to pick them up from the ticket office was that I would not be seeing my *friend* for a couple of days.

Celia had the cheek to phone me the next day, to thank me for treating her and Jamie. I nearly burst at that – he was the bastard who'd booked them for me.

I did, of course, learn from that experience by acknowledging that I had no friends, only acquaintances according to their usefulness. Still abide by it to this day!

They got engaged the following month, but I didn't get an invitation to the party. Wouldn't have gone anyway.

They never did get married though. Jamie had a crash in his MG sports car shortly after the engagement. The papers reported that someone had cut partly through the brake fluid line. He always did drive erratically anyway.

Celia was supposed to have been with him. They were going to Wimbledon to watch the finals. Unfortunately, she had food poisoning, so the obnoxious Jamie died alone.

Perhaps I should brush up on toxins. Too late for Celia now though.

I should have had that car – I should have had Celia and all her money.

Whatever! I must now think about someone else to be my chattel.

~

Georgina was next on my list. She was a few months older than me and already had her BSc. (Hons). One very clever lady was Georgina, probably on a par with me, which makes her a formidable companion. She is very into smart dressy clothes, worn with three-inch stilettos – I like! Only slightly shorter than me, she is tall for a woman. Her figure is pretty good, even though she hasn't much in the boob department. Perhaps her shoulders are a little wide but it's difficult to tell because she likes to wear smart suits with shoulder pads and shirt-blouses, which she sometimes wears with a tie. However, she has long legs, and I can at least be sure that her calves and ankles are pretty neat. I might be able to judge the rest later.

I decided to wine and dine her, and to arrive on time. The cow kept me waiting for half an hour and I found it very difficult to produce my lady-killer smile. Anyway, it proved to be a very enjoyable evening. We had much in common, both intellectually and professionally. We loved opera, hated golf and enjoyed good food. I also soon learnt that she abhorred the fuss with wine tasting, so I just told the waiter to stick the bottle on the table and we would drink it. We did too, and another one as well, plus brandy with our coffee.

Later, I walked her home and was invited in for a drink. That was another surprise. I was not aware that she had her own flat. It was large and comfortable, apparently furnished by devoted parents as a reward for graduating with honours.

We listened to various opera highlights and enthusiastically discussed the orchestras, the conductors and the singers, whilst imbibing a very passable Irish whiskey. Georgina obviously likes her liquor and can hold it well. However, alcohol does tend to loosen the tongue and I eventually learnt why she was also unsuited to be my wife.

She had just informed me that she preferred to be called George when I heard a key turning in the front door. Georgina jumped up and flung herself into the arms of the person who entered the room. They hugged and kissed for a while then, looking very flushed and pretty, Georgina found time to introduce her friend to me.

"This is Victoria," she said. "Vicky is a doctor and she's just finished a twenty-hour stint at the Royal."

We shook hands. God, she was gorgeous. Even wearing flat shoes, I could tell her legs were good. She had what I can only describe as 'a jolly derrière;' a narrow waist and the sort of bust I would like to bury my head between.

"It's good of you to entertain George for me. She gets lonely when I'm on duty. Thank you."

She even possessed a sexy voice.

I guess I must have given some suitable reply, but I can't remember what it was, and soon after took my leave of them.

Bloody dikes!

That was another one down the drain.

~

Somewhere in between the ensuing eighteen months, I had found employment with a chemical research company, which, with my qualifications and magnificent demeanour, was comparatively easy. I was given a small laboratory all to myself, where I could work on special projects.

Impressive, eh!

Anyway, that was where I got myself some interesting experiences with the girl who delivered the mail and ran messages. Her name was Sharon.

~

Sharon was petite, without the impression I receive from that word, of one who is a small, dainty person of quality. Whilst she was undoubtedly small and dainty, with a mass of blond curls bouncing around an elfin face, she was just about as common as you can get. She wore her miniskirts just that little bit shorter than other women and her tops a little more revealing of perfectly rounded breasts. The high slender heels of her shoes were bright red, the soles adhering to narrow feet by means of thin straps, fastened above shapely ankles with buckled straps.

She looked a dream, providing she kept her mouth shut. That voice! It was the typical rasp of a smoker, but not just hard – it was loud. I mean LOUD! It was coarse too. Every 'H' hitting the ground before it could possibly be enunciated, every word ending with a 'T' clipped and wherever able the 'th' sound was also dropped. But the vocal sounds emitting from those delightful kissable lips were not the only discrepancy of that body-part, for Sharon did not chew, she chomped at her food, sounding like a pig at the trough. More unfortunate – she perpetually chewed gum.

The small laboratory I named The Hovel (that sign replacing the one carrying my name) sported a loft, which I found I could reach by standing on a lab stool and pulling myself upwards. The muscles in my arms, of course, are incredibly strong. I had acquired a straw bail and spread it over the boards to form a place to lay with Sharon, who was ready, willing and extremely able.

I shall never know where she got such amazing sexual experience. Surely it could not be doing what came naturally, although natural is certainly the way it seemed. I enjoyed these experiences nearly every weekday for all the time I worked at the Research Centre, right up to that day the bastards sacked me.

She was quite something. I soon banned chewing gum and prevented her from talking by keeping my lips firmly pressed against hers. However, there was no way I could take her as a wife…so I must proceed with my search.

~

I finally found Miss Right whilst still consorting regularly with Sharon.

~

My Suzanne was small, petite even, almost pretty, with thick dark shining hair flowing down to her waist. Her eyes were a dark brown that gazed at yours truly, with the adoration of a Newfoundland puppy. She could dance too, which is where I first discovered her, and carefully pursued her for more than a year. I needed to do that, although it went against the grain for me because she was only sixteen years old and was still at school. I was, at that time, ten years older than Suzanne and knew for a fact that she was a totally virginal innocent.

Her father regularly acted as master of ceremonies for the monthly dance at a local ballroom. These affairs were not bad and were a good place to find unattached women, of whom there were usually at least half a dozen that regularly danced together for lack of male partners. Dress at these dances was optional, but I decided to go clothed. *Sorry, my ready wit is still able to break loose occasionally.* Suzanne's parents invariably wore full evening dress, but she was usually dressed like a little kid in her Sunday best.

I, of course, always arrived late. My timing was impeccable, just in time to ask Suzanne for the dance prior to a break for refreshments. I would then take her with me to purchase disgusting coffee and a cake, returning to my seat at the edge of the ballroom, as far away from the fond parents as possible. She remained with me for the rest of the evening, during which I learned what I could and plied her with charm. During the last waltz, I left her at her parent's table before the end, grabbed my outdoor shoes and was on my way home before it finished. That is always a good ploy, she wonders if she will see me next month and her parents will try to turn her against me. They never did like me, didn't understand me of course. After all, they are boring, normal people.

Suzanne took my advice, of course, and duly left her private school without taking the exams that would have undoubtedly got her a university place. As it was, she obtained a post with a firm of solicitors, which served to expand her non-existing knowledge as to how the other half lived.

I spent two years breaking her in, at the end of which she was my obedient slave, not daring to cross me for fear of losing her handsome boyfriend. I introduced her to my penis, of which she seemed to be terrified. This was when I realised for the first time that Suzanne had no knowledge whatsoever of the differences between the bodies of men and women, let alone sex. So it was that it became necessary for me to explain to her the facts of life. Poor kid, but I promised not to make the male/female engagement until such time as we might be married. However, I did make it quite clear that I expected petting, to quite a considerable degree, to which she agreed on the grounds that if she loved me, she would naturally be prepared to 'go nearly all the way.'

Things got more interesting from that point. We would spend the whole of a Sunday together, having told her mother that we were meeting friends to go to various places. In fact, we mostly found ourselves a quiet secluded spot and settled down for the rest of the day with a picnic, flasks of coffee and bottles of fizzy drinks. Sometimes we would build a hide with bent branches covered with ferns and suchlike. In very chilly weather, we burrowed into the hay in a barn attached to the farm of one farmer or another. I often wonder what one of them thought when he discovered the bright red and green skirt that somehow got lost amongst his hay. She had to arrive home at a time her parents were not likely to open the front door. Her legs must have been frozen, bare as they were.

It was alongside a lake in the grounds of some large estate attached to a mansion that I broke her maidenhead. No, I kept my word – always do. I used an item manufactured from a cold resin process I had invented, the mould being a laboratory tube. She fussed a bit but was soon brought under control, and although I don't think she got much out of the experience, I very much enjoyed the whole operation. I recall considering the next step, progressively larger diameter – bottles could be interesting.

I clearly remember the first occasion I was obliged to inflict physical punishment on her. I had made the coffee, to which had been added copious amounts of sugar, just as I like it. She took a sip, said "Ugh" and threw the precious brew to the ground. I removed my belt, put her over my knees and thwacked her soundly. She, of course, blubbered, whereupon I drew her tenderly to me and explained her foolishness. She promised never again to be so wicked, and all was forgiven. I believe in instant punishment, followed by the offender's repentance and my gracious forgiveness.

Anyway, sometime later, I decided we should be married and being a gentleman bought her an engagement ring and went to tell her parents the great news. It is hard to imagine, but her father had the temerity to tell me he was not happy to see his daughter marrying me. What on earth did he expect for her – a bloody duke? He seemed not to appreciate the great honour I was doing his miserable family, by allowing a union between it and the superior Deville dynasty. So, I told him straight.

"If you refuse to willingly allow us to marry, I will make sure your daughter is pregnant, then you will be only too pleased to give us you're blessing."

The stupid little twerp said, "I do not like you, Michael. You are rude and inordinately arrogant. However, if Suzanne still wishes to marry you in one year's time, when she is nineteen, then I will not stand in your way."

And that's the way it was.

Then it was time for her to meet my parents. Suzanne and my mother tolerated each other in a polite manner but my father adored her. He had nicknames for everyone, mine being Mackerel, no I have no idea why, but Suzanne became Sprat Marigold. It takes a sprat to catch a mackerel. Boom! Boom!

So, we were married and just one year later I was banished from the Research Centre. (*Yes, at that time I did still frolic with Sharon, completely unknown to my wife*). I must say that Suzanne was completely supportive and got herself a secretarial job to support the pair of us, whilst I kept looking for suitable employment. That took nearly another year and all that time we said nothing of the situation to our families, despite our financial difficulties.

I cannot say ours was a happy marriage, but so far as the rest of humanity was concerned it was ideal, as neither of us had the inclination to wash our dirty linen in public. This state lasted until I met Helena Rose some twenty-five years later.

~

That seemed to be the end of the session, which appeared to be filled with memories covering several years. The remainder of the typing on the memory-stick was in italics, which Michael tended to use when differentiating between something within his reality, rather than what he refers to as MMM.

~

What you choose to use of the final 'wifie' story is entirely up to you, Suzanne, but I feel it is imperative that I tell all currently.

I have always had my hobbies, such as model railways, which you, Suzanne, always followed supportively along with me, if not willingly then without any argument. You typed letters to other enthusiasts for me, made models and produced rubber moulds manufactured from coal, for mountains. Tagging along as you had always done throughout our marriage, knowing that to do so kept the peace, kept me happy, which, after all, was always of paramount importance.

I invariably regretted it after the necessity of punishing you, but I was always most careful to make sure punches were aimed at your soft breasts or somewhere on the body where bruises could not be seen.

Now here I am, a prisoner within my own aching body, and I sincerely regret my treatment of you, Suzanne, more than ever before. You will see that memories I would rather have left buried have been forced to my knowledge. I now realise your true value, not only as a wife but also as a human being. If you were here, I'd feel stronger, safer.

The MMM is a mixture of excitement and regret, especially where you are concerned, Suzanne. Could it be that I am being given time to repent my past – if so, I certainly do so regarding my treatment of you. Other things? Maybe – maybe not. However, I am still not sure where the episodes with the psychiatrist fit. Certainly, some of that time is prior to my actual birth but, he appears during my late teens/twenties.

Oh, God! These memories are for me a trip through Hell, and I know for sure that it is a hell created by myself...

~

It was Citizens Band Radio that finally did it for us wasn't it, Suzanne? The first and only thing that you flatly refused to become involved in.

At the time it started its popularity the radio band was illegal, which of course, is what drew me to it in the first place. Helena Rose was one of the people to whom I spoke. One evening I recall clearly, there was a deep discussion concerning Extra Sensory Perception. I went by the name of Gilpin, if you remember, and she introduced herself as Mystic Lady. The atmosphere was charismatic, and I felt a pleasant sensation sweep through my body. This woman was magical. We spoke together most evenings until eventually a meeting was arranged (an 'eyeball'). I ordered you to accompany me and you dared to voice your feelings about the visit and to give an opinion of the exciting woman that you'd never even spoken to. Very unwise! It ensured your future as a 'chaperone' to my new ladylove.

New, but not the first by a long chalk. I had mostly kept all my alliances safely from you and it was not until I became involved with CB radio that I decided it would be fun to openly humiliate you. Do you remember how I would take you to dances or parties and flirt outrageously with other women?

On more than one occasion, I recall fondling another woman in front of you, Suzanne, and suggesting you joined us too. This period was not much fun though as you would sit quietly until I indicated that it was time to go home, then in your maddening manner, you would wish our hostess goodbye and retreat to the car. So, I tended to back off this game until I met Helena Rose (Mystic Lady) and fell hopelessly in lust with her.

Helena Rose had at some time between the birthing of her numerous daughters, found time to study psychology. Although unqualified, she was pretty good and combined with my own turn of mind we made a formidable team.

What we did to Suzanne, both psychologically and physically, was amazing. It got so she knew at some point she would be removed from my life one way or another and that scared her, which was the object of the exercise. That was when I learnt my wife had more to her than I had thought possible. One day in the second week of March, when I had decided to give her the pleasure of my company for the evening, she dropped her bombshell.

"I've bought myself a house and will be moving on the 23rd of this month. Do close your mouth Michael, you look foolish."

The bitch had gone behind my back and bought a bloody house. But that was not all…

"I shall need you to help me move – you, not her. I also require a divorce. It's up to you how you manage it. We can do it the easy way, irreconcilable behaviour on your part, after a friendly separation of two years, or I can drag you and her through the mill of adultery, fornication and the rest."

"Don't be ridiculous," I told her. "I would have you on your knees in very short order."

That was when you told me how over the past six months, you had secretly made recordings of our conversations. Not only those though, but you had also actually recorded Helena Rose and me during our 'games' with you. These you had apparently duplicated; one copy having been given to your doctor the other enclosed in an envelope addressed to a solicitor friend. This was apparently locked in your desk at work with instructions that it should be passed to him, should you meet an untimely death, or disappear.

Game set and match to Suzanne.

I bought the furniture and carpets, helped you move, and deposited several thousand pounds to your account.

Helena Rose moved in with me, on the understanding that none of her six daughters would ever enter my home. I'm not quite certain what arrangements she made, I was, still am, not interested. Once I leave this mortal coil, I don't know what she will do, but I swear I'll haunt her if she disobeys my ruling. Poor cow. She thought she was going to have all the goodies that Suzanne had with none of the unhappiness. She had it all – in spades. It's my money she likes but I didn't give her the chance to get her hands on it. I provide her with housing and food but any perks she wants must be earned. To this end, she obtained employment and relies on my generosity when she pleases me.

Then this damned disease happened, and it was in the early stages that I remembered my visits to the psychiatrist Dr Jennings/Dracula all those years ago. I'd almost forgotten about him. So, one day with Helena Rose at work and not having the energy to play trains…

That was what you, Suzanne, used to say behind my back. "Michael's playing trains…"

…I looked for any papers I might have retained in the box at the back of my train-room cupboard but there are very few and those will be retained in the box with anything else I contrive. Did I throw some things away when you left me, Suzanne, or did you have a grand clear out one day? Never mind, I settled down with a cup of tea. I've got this a bit out of sequence here, but it is as things occur to me that I must get them down in case I forget. I would not have forgotten before this disease hit me, but nowadays I am not quite sure. The only thing I know I can guarantee full recollection of is when I come out of my Magic Memory Mode. But each new MMM experience seems to obliterate the previous one and my only way of keeping things in order is to get them on the computer so I can read what happens. As time passes, I'm getting more scared. I have no real recollection of breaking into the psychiatrist's premises, but undoubtedly, I did, his notes about me are in the box and I can only assume that the regressions must bear a resemblance to what really happened. I am not sure, don't know what is real and what is not! However, bits I do clearly remember as having happened, such as seeking a suitable wife and everything connected with you, Suzanne.

Am I mad? I'm scared!

Suzanne's Notes

I was rather shocked by the foregoing, especially where it applied to myself. Perhaps he had been genuinely sorry towards the end, it does appear so. I hope he repented and was given Heavenly Grace. On the other hand, he always had the ability to make me feel that way. He knew I would forgive if not forget, but I can never forgive his treatment of me or his arrogance regarding other women.

He jumped from speaking to me directly, to telling it as he remembered, treating me as just one of his women. At one time I would have been deeply upset, now I didn't care, but was nevertheless intrigued as to what might follow.

The memory stick had no more on it, so I printed a hard copy and replaced MS number two. I'd had enough for the time being.

~

I feel no inclination to check out the various potential applicants for the situation of 'wifie' to my ex-husband and was fully aware of the various paramours involved during our marriage. There had been a woman with the Great Danes who lived in a caravan and whose husband was a night-worker. The dogs had superior premises to those occupied by their owner, except for one who shared the accommodation, ensuring the layer of short dog hairs that covered virtually everything. She was busty and more than willing to be available – I was not!

But that is immaterial, and I decided to check out Dr Jennings. The Clinic, however, was no longer operative, having closed when the area was refurbished. Some thirty years had passed since that time and no one in the area could even remember the man I was seeking.

So, I started looking for the delectable Debra Dennison, a task that turned out to be easier than I could imagine. I perused the telephone directory looking for the name of Dennison. After all, if she had not run off with her brother-in-law the name would be the same. There were about twenty to thirty entries, not all spelt the same way, but only three with the initial D and only one entered as *Dennison Debra*. I noted the address in a nearby town and pondered as to whether I should telephone her or just make a house call. No. That would not be polite, so I considered my story and dialled the number.

It rang only three times before a pleasant voice said, "Hello." Mmm! She was obviously used to receiving unwanted cold calls and was giving nothing away.

I said, "I am so sorry to bother you, but I am writing a biography of a psychiatrist by the name of Dr Jennings, and I wondered if you might be the Debra Dennison who worked for him when the practice was in the City Centre? I do apologise if I have the wrong person…" I drew it out a bit, hoping she would help and fill the gap. She did.

"Oh yes! I worked for him back then – how can I help?"

We continued speaking for a few more minutes during which we arranged that I would call on her at home the next day, in time for coffee at ten o'clock.

When I arrived and rang the bell, Debra opened the door and proved not to be the plain, overweight woman I was expecting, but a comfortable person in her late sixties, with a welcoming smile. She was wearing a floral printed dress in bright yellow, with a beige cardigan and open sandals.

The house was the end one of a small terrace of six, all painted white with brightly painted doors and window frames and small, neat pocket-handkerchief, front gardens. A shining red car was parked under a covered carport at the side of the house, and I assumed that any cars belonging to owners of the four middle properties were either parked on the road or on the land that fronted their homes.

Debra led me through a long narrow passageway, carpeted the same as that covering the stairs that led up from the right-hand side. No hair shedding animals here and not any sign of dirt, so probably no children. We entered a comfortable kitchen attractively appointed with light oak cabinets and a small gate-leg table with one leaf open and just two matching chairs. It smelled of flowers and coffee with an underlying aroma of buttered toast. A large window gave a view of the long narrow garden that looked as neat and well vacuumed as the house, and with the beautiful display of rose bushes and bed flowers, I was sure it smelled just as good.

"Shall we take our coffee in the garden?"

"That would be lovely. What a gorgeous garden you have, do you tend it yourself?"

We chatted in this manner for a while then Debra said, "So what is it you want to know about the Doctor?"

I withdrew the faithful notebook from my bag and prepared to take notes.

"Was he a good boss? Was he well-liked by his colleagues and patients?"

Debra closed her eyes, thinking back, "I was good at my job. I was well paid and had a fair amount of time to myself, so was able to keep everything well organised, which was what the Doctor expected of me. There was a small kitchen where I could make a hot drink." She shrugged and gave a small, tight smile. "Coffee usually, but the Doctor never drank coffee, or tea for that matter, he kept some sort of red wine in his office, in dark bottles. They were in a locked cupboard in his room, and I only ever saw one of them once." She shuddered. "The label was black and the name on it was in red, like dripping blood, but he hustled it out of sight as soon as I entered the room. The wine in his glass though made me think of blood too."

She shuddered again. "That was the only time he ever shouted at me. '*Don't you dare to ever enter my office again until you hear me bid you to come in. Do you understand me, Mrs Dennison?*' He always called me Mrs Dennison, although I never married – I always called him Doctor."

I made no comment and waited for her to continue.

"That was the only time in five years. Amazing, isn't it? I was there all that time, and I never once had a personal conversation with him. I made appointments, saw patients were comfortable and made them a drink if they would need to wait a while before he was ready. I did the filing and lived my own life."

She stopped again, obviously thinking over the letters Michael had found and read, and the life she had been able to live within her own bubble. I wondered if 'the Doctor' was aware of her double life – he'd probably been the catalyst. No wonder Mike had referred to him as Dracula. But my main reason for visiting Debra was to find out about a certain patient, and it was now time to move in that direction.

"What about his patients, Debra? Did they ever talk to you about him? Did he use hypnotism on them?"

"I'm not sure I should talk about that. Of course, I knew who he saw but he kept some things to himself. I did the main filing, but he kept bits and pieces in his own system and I know he had a recorder. It was kept in the middle drawer of his desk and operated by buttons that looked like decorations on the front of it."

"How did you come to know about that, Debra?"

"The Doctor had been seeing this man. He only came half a dozen times but one day the door hadn't been closed properly and I heard what sounded like the voice of a child. Well, I was curious, naturally. You would have been too. Anyway, I peeped through the crack and only the two of them were in there. Then my office door opened, and the draught made the Doctor's door click shut. I don't think he heard anything, never said a word to me anyway. It was a Friday and the Doctor always pushed off as soon as the afternoon appointment was finished, usually about a quarter to four. I used to leave him time to get away, then locked up and left. That day, I snooped around his room. Everything was locked up, but I guessed he had been recording, it's the natural thing to do when somebody's regressing. I looked for the tape recorder but there was nothing to be seen. Then, sitting in his chair I could see the knobbly decoration on the desk drawer and realised that they were too sticking out, you know – not sort of rounded and set deep as you'd expect. I didn't dare press one, but it did look like that's what it was for, just enough for me to know what it was. That patient was a bit of a charmer, a flirt."

She blushed. "I think he fancied me."

She told me about other patients, their odd ways and foibles, and I listened and made the right sounds but had heard what I needed to. Michael had been to see Dr Jennings and Debra had corroborated what he had said (*the answer came in the voice of a tearful ten-year-old boy*).

I left as soon as I could politely do so, after all, I had instigated the interview and Debra had been very cooperative.

~

Having confirmed the first part of Michael's strange story, I could now continue.

Setting aside what I have already perused, I shall need to clear my head completely of what has gone and apply an open mind to what must follow. I shall insert any notes I may make in sequence.

It was another couple of weeks before I once again opened the box and inserted the next disc into my laptop…

Michael had started with one of his letters, prior to regressing; what he called his reality zone.

~

I am about to relax into the MMM, Suzanne. I do not know what it will reveal this time, maybe more than half-remembered things but maybe something altogether different.

If I come through this next experience, I will dub it as Item #3.

I have set my alarm to ring in two hours, in the hope that it will wake me and draw me back into the present. If not…well, what can I say? I trust this MMM will continue; partly from mere curiosity and partly so I can record the effects of regression. Perhaps it will reveal a side of psychology, or maybe a part of the human brain not yet discovered

Part 2
Peter De Ville Twentieth Century
Circa 1912–1925

1

Item #3

This was the place I first met him. Right here, sitting on the grass hump of a grave, leaning against the north wall of the cemetery. As far away from the Rectory as possible, but still within the boundaries of St Patrick's, my father's church. I needed to think.

Mother had died of tuberculosis when I was just three and since then I'd only had the companionship of my father and older brother, John. John was six years older than me and, on the occasions, he was home from boarding school, had little time for a kid brother. The only female influence in my life was our housekeeper/cook, Gwyneth Jones. She was a kind body who made sure I was properly clothed and fed and patched up my cuts and bruises when I fell whilst picking the best apples at the top of the tree. When I was seven, I was sent off to boarding school, where the only female was Matron who performed much the same tasks as Gwyneth Jones.

I didn't like my father very much; I didn't understand him in those days I suppose. He was always serious, a good man who saw everything in black or white; you know, nothing in between, just good or bad. He was always strict, but when I think about it, was never actually unfair. Anyway, it was the week after my eighteenth birthday when he called me into his study and informed me that it had been decided I should follow in his footsteps, and ultimately be indoctrinated into the church.

Just like that – my future had been decided for me with no consultation. It was assumed, naturally, that was his decree then so be it. But I didn't want to go into the dull serious church, to which I had been dragged (mentally anyway) for as long as I could remember. However, since my elder brother had qualified as a doctor, married his childhood sweetheart and moved away from the precincts of St Patrick's, I spent a great deal of time reading, daydreaming and thinking. I had no desire for the boring country pursuits, and to me, the equally boring church life of choir, jumble sales, fetes and suchlike. No, I wanted to broaden my horizons not only in the British Isles but abroad.

When I spoke of this to my father, his response was that I could probably achieve that through the ministry missions, preaching to the ungodly, in places like Africa and the jungles of South America.

"You don't understand," I yelled at him, and ran from the study.

How could I expect him to understand? I was a red-blooded young man of eighteen and one week, with all the pubescent desires of my species; he had never seen the books and magazines I had acquired from a second-hand bookshop in the city. He would have had a fit had he done so; in fact, I doubt he believed such pleasures existed.

It was just then that a shadow engulfed me, and I looked up to see a figure towering above me. From my position on the ground with my back against the wall, he looked eight feet tall. I started to stand but he indicated with a gentle touch to my shoulder to remain where I was and folded his thin gangling body to sit beside me. He wore all black, like the garb such as clergymen wear, but with a crimson collar replacing the usual white. His hair was dark and slicked tight to his head, a widow's peak clearly defined, with not a hair out of place.

"Young man," he said, "you are strong and adventurous, why do you not join the Army where you can do good for your countrymen, travel and gain experience, before settling down? The choice should be yours – follow in your father's rather tedious footsteps or be guided by me to a very different life."

I tried to speak, ask questions, but he silenced me with a wave of his hand.

"Should you decide to take the second course then you must promise this."

He stared into my eyes and his, dark, deep-set, seemed to be suffused in a red glow. I screwed up my eyes to try and clear my now throbbing head, then nodded, which he appeared to accept as the affirmative.

"You will say nothing of this meeting, never under any circumstances should you speak of me. You will return to the Rectory, collect what is necessary, and make your way to the train station, where you will take the 1.30 train to London. On arrival, you will ask for directions to the Army Recruitment Offices and there, you will join the army. Should I at any time require it, you will immediately think of 'The Man in Black' and come to me, whatever your circumstances at the time."

He stopped me from asking a question, raising his hand and saying, "You will know without a doubt, but if you fail to obey, then grievous retribution will fall upon you."

He stood up and scared now, I followed his lead as if yanked by an invisible rope. This action appeared to please and amuse him and smiling, the grin of a crocodile, he grasped my hand shaking it firmly, and saying nothing further strode away behind the church towards the old lych-gate. I watched for him to pass through it and onto the road, but although I stayed there for perhaps fifteen minutes, he never appeared, and much water had flowed under the bridge before I was to meet him again.

I don't remember how much time passed since this strange experience but eventually, I made my way back to the Rectory. I entered through the kitchen door and ascended to my room via the back stairs. I stood for a while taking in the familiar objects, only a few of which I really cared for anymore. The photo of my dead mother, with my father and brother, myself a mere baby, held lovingly in her arms. I gazed at it, trying to imagine that time when we were still a proper family. What would my life have been like if she had been there? Yes, the photo would come with me, so I wrapped it carefully in the scarf Gwyneth Jones had knitted for me as a present last Christmas. My fob watch was an eighteenth birthday present from my father. It was a good one but only silver, not gold like the one he had given John on his eighteenth. I recognised the jealousy trying to creep into my mind and pushed it out, returning the watch to my pocket.

I sorted out half a dozen books from my secret store, hidden behind the great tomes of encyclopaedias and various religious books. Only one of these tomes had ever held any true fascination for me, and that was, *Fox's Book of Martyrs*. I loved to read of the terrible tortures inflicted upon people who had different views from those of the dreaded Inquisition. I confess it turned me on – yes it did, really.

The cleaner only came in three times a week and I had seen her cleaning practices – a flick and a promise, was what she called it, always promising herself and anyone else listening, that she would give it a 'proper do' next time. I knew it was most unlikely she would ever find my store of 'other' books and wasn't particularly worried if she did. I shook my head, trying to clear it of both the pensive thoughts and throbbing pain. First, I tackled the pain and took three aspirin tablets with water, then set about gathering what would fit into my carpetbag. To those items previously mentioned, I added two changes of underclothes, three clean shirts, a washbag and my shaving equipment. That latter item was not strictly necessary, as I only needed to shave perhaps once a week. But if I was to join the army and travel, then for sure I would need it as I matured.

I debated just disappearing, but my father's careful and correct upbringing pushed that away. So it was that I sat down and wrote the note that was to cause the speedy decline of his health, and subsequent death only six months after my departure.

Dear Father,

I am sorry but I find it impossible to accept your decision for my future and have decided to go forth into the world to seek travel and adventure.

By the time you find this, I will have joined the army and be in training to fight for the rights and protection of my country. Once the papers are signed then the die is cast. Please do not attempt to contact me, for my mind is made up and to try and extricate me from that contract can only cause the ultimate breakdown of our relationship.

I am sorry, Father, if I cause you grief but will write to you regularly, if possible and the next time we meet I will be wearing a uniform.

Please think kindly of me and forgive your son,

Peter.

Placing it in the centre of my dismal dark blue bedspread, I left the house the way I entered, collected my bicycle from the outbuilding and cycled the five or so miles to the station. Leaving the cycle with the station guard I bought a single ticket to London, and at 1.30 pm sharp I was on my way.

At Victoria Station, I found someone able to direct me to my next destination, and after walking for fifteen minutes I entered the Army Recruitment Office, declared myself to be eighteen, signed the appropriate papers and joined a queue of other young men to await a medical. This entailed a wait of an hour, followed by a very thorough medical examination, which I passed with flying colours. Having attended a boarding school I was used to appearing naked in front of other males, but I must confess that the doctor cupping my testicles whilst I coughed, caused me blushing embarrassment.

That over, I was herded with my companions to a ramshackle army vehicle, in which we were transported to an initial training camp, where for the next month, we were drilled, exercised, taught to fire guns and use bayonets. The sergeant was quite a decent chap, large of stature, with a round head and loud of speech, but I thought most of the officers were total prats who considered themselves way above the privates. The only true advantage they had was their wealthy background, which, in all honesty, was not that much different from my own. I kept quiet about that though and soon made friends amongst the men with whom I was billeted.

I wrote to both my father and brother at the end of the first week, determined to do so *every* week until such time as we should meet again. However, I never received any replies so at the end of my second month's training I ceased trying to communicate. Then, on a cold, dark, rainy and thoroughly miserable day at the beginning of December, we were marched to the station where we boarded a train for Southampton. It was another march in the pouring rain and fully laden with kit bags, guns and ammunition, of a mile or so from the station to the docks, where we embarked aboard a ship and set sail for France, thus entering the darkest period of my life to date.

~

The trenches were deep, wet and muddy, with the smell of ammunition, blood and death permeating through them. I heard gunfire and howls of pain, saw men, some of them my friends, fall injured. Some lost arms, some legs, some their precious sight, and overall, I thought perhaps those dead were the lucky ones. I made several attempts to drag injured men to safety and to my shame, shot men of my own age who were trying to shoot me. Did these men not have fathers, and if they were lucky, mothers too? Some would have wives and maybe children of their own. How could it possibly be that young men who should be laughing and playing games together were facing each other in war? Just because someone of great authority said it should be thus and the officers ordered them to the killing fields of Europe. Had some of those foreigners left home in the same manner as I had done? What a very sad situation!

Our platoon was now reduced to only eight men, three of whom were seriously injured, and our communications equipment was defunct. But no matter what risks I took, it seemed as though bullets aimed in my direction were deflected before they reached their target. In this way, I acquired the name of Lucky Pete, which was how my superior officer came to choose me to run across the battlefield with a message, explaining our situation and asking for help.

I had just reached the protection of a small wood when through my mind went the phrase, *The Man in Black*. Immediately, I realised that the strange creature that I had encountered in the graveyard of my father's church was calling me. What was it he had said?

"Should I at any time require it, you will immediately come to me, whatever your circumstances at the time."
"Come now – it is time – I require you."

I felt his pull but my sense of duty to my comrades was stronger, and although I knew full well that our bargain required my immediate obedience whatever my circumstances, I ignored his call and ran on to complete my task.

The officer in charge was a considerate man and insisted that I sat in his presence, instructing his batman to make tea and ensure it contained sugar. This substance was not usually available to the ranks, and I appreciated his gentlemanly action greatly. However, although he prevailed upon me to stay with his own platoon and re-join my own in their company, I insisted on returning within the hour to inform those few besieged men that relief was on the way.

As I entered the same wood on my return journey, he was standing just under the cover of the trees. His face was consumed with an anger that frightened me, and his eyes locked on mine, glowing with that crimson light I had seen before.

"Why did you not obey?"

He spoke in almost a whisper, but I heard every letter, every nuance, and trembled.

"Well?"

I tried to drop my eyes from his glare but could not.
"I…I…I had my duty to perform for my platoon, their very existence depended on my carrying it out successfully."

"Precisely. Their existence depended on you – a duty you should have failed to complete – the death of every single member of that regiment except for yourself, Lucky Pete."

He spoke with deep sarcasm, and I realised at that moment that I had made a deal with the devil and although he thought he owned my very soul, my strong Christian upbringing had given me the protection of God. As I understood, I broke my gaze from his and said firmly, "Get thou behind me Satan in the name of the Father, Son and Holy Ghost."

He roared. I cannot express it in writing, only that he roared like some huge wild animal.

"You will live to regret your folly, young man. You may be Lucky Pete but that applies only to your person and not to those for whom you have regard."

And with that, he retreated backwards and appeared to disintegrate into the trees themselves.

My running mission did, in fact, serve to save the remnants of my platoon and gradually, through the various deaths amongst officers over the next year, I found myself promoted rapidly.

2

At the end of April 1917, I received a letter from my brother John, informing me of the death of our father, on the 23rd of March 1917, due apparently to a heart attack. He had been found lying in front of the altar in his church, with the large silver cross that always stood upon it clasped firmly in his hands. I was offered compassionate leave but as the funeral had naturally already taken place, I refused.

However, I was given leave over the Christmas period of 1917 and returned to Britain where I spent the holiday with my brother and his wife. They had been married for four years now and at last; they were expecting the happy event of their firstborn. The child was born on Christmas Eve, a weak and ailing boy who was speedily christened Noel and died on Boxing Day. His mother, who had lost much blood, followed her son just one week later. My brother was devastated, Margaret had been his childhood sweetheart and they had a deep abiding love, which had shown in their daily lives.

This time I applied for and received compassionate leave for a further week and was able to attend my second funeral in just six days. John's need for me was obvious. I was his only living relative and Margaret, an only child, had been orphaned at the age of twelve.

That night, I dreamed about *him*. I *will not* enunciate the words that call me to him. He smiled evilly as he informed me that he had now taken the souls of my father, sister-in-law and nephew as revenge for my failure to obey his call.

He also said in that ghastly whispering voice, *"Only one to go for the time being."*

~

I returned to my regiment in France, now a captain, and for the next year fought the enemy and watched more of my companions die whilst I miraculously survived.

~

Then I met Angelique. She was the youngest daughter of the farmer on whose land we were entrenched, and she was beautiful as an angel, with blond curls, deep blue eyes, full lips shaped like Cupid's bow and a cute retroussé nose. All the men loved her, but I was the one whose love was returned, and in April 1918 we were married in the local church.

I now corresponded with my brother on a regular monthly basis, but when I failed to hear from him prior to my marriage, of which forthcoming event I informed him by letter during the first week of March, I felt considerably concerned. I consequently wrote to the hospital in Manchester where he was employed, asking for information concerning my brother. A response was received more promptly than expected and it contained news of John's death on the 16th of January 1918. He had apparently been found hanging in the hospital mortuary. A suicide note was found on the gurney beside him, reading:

My brother's forthcoming marriage brings the loss of my own true love, together with that of our child Noel, so close to mind that I cannot bear to continue with life. As Peter marries and fertilises the eggs of his wife, I wish them much happiness.
I am sorry,

John Martin de Ville.

The hospital staff had not known of my whereabouts, except that I was a captain in the army, based somewhere in France. My letter enabled them to respond immediately.

That night, the man of evil appeared in my dreams once again. He was of great good humour and evil intent, shaking a finger at me and saying, *"Another one down."* That crocodile grimaces. *"Now you must considerately supply me with more."*

I knew full well of what he spoke and trembled in fear and anger, but I also knew he would take his revenge in full, as he had first threatened.

~

The death of my wife occurred sooner than I could have ever expected. At the end of July 1918, a German regiment stormed her father's farm, where she and I now resided. They shot Monsieur Trebuchet and the two farm workers, then raped and shot Madame Trebuchet in front of her daughter; finally taking turns to assault my wife before shooting her too. I discovered my family that night, and had I not known her dear body so well I could not have recognised Angelique, as those devils had shot her in the face, totally obliterating those dear, beautiful features. They had also murdered our child within her.

3

That was when I finally broke, both mentally and physically. I insisted on arranging and attending the funerals of my wife and parents-in-law, who had loved me like a son, after which I recall very little. Only that I was returned in the company of a doctor and nurse, to England.

By the time I recovered my senses, I had been in the Priory Hospital for mentally affected service patients for several months, and the war was over. I was returning to health, to the extent that I decided to avail myself of my psychiatrist's suggestion, to write down those details of my life, which disturb my peace of mind. It was not an easy task. The writing came easily enough, but the remembering saddened me, and I spent much time in unmanly tears. I frequently asked myself for what reason and for whom I cry. Can it be self-pity, or for those I have lost? But when I consider it, I realise that the dead have no need of my sorrow, they were now surely released from their suffering. Yes, that must be it, my tears were for myself, my great loss.

That was when I fell into a deep, exhausted sleep and *he* called me to him for the second time. In my dream, I remembered the words, *The Man in Black,* and immediately heard his voice saying…

"Come to me – come into the grounds by the lake – come now!"

This time I had only myself to lose, so rising from my bed I made my way out of the open glass doors, into the garden, across the grass towards the ornamental lake. He was there, arms akimbo, standing tall and straight, his crimson collar loosely comfortable around his scraggy neck.

"So, have you learnt your lesson, young man and come to receive instructions from your Master? Those for whom you had much regard, I suppose you would say loved, all are gone, Peter de Ville."

That deep, whispering voice, filled with hatred and sarcasm, riled me beyond words, but he continued.

"They are now members of my own community," again that sarcastic satisfaction, *"and will remain so for all eternity. Now is the time for you to join them in the deep chasm of the deepest abyss."*

He laughed then. A harsh, foul sound, full of evil wickedness.

"I think not," said I, stepping swiftly towards him and withdrawing from my pocket the sharp knife I had secreted there. Not stopping to consider my actions I drew the blade across his throat above the crimson collar, causing it to only darken as blood flowed.

He looked somewhat surprised by my action and slowly crumbled to the edge of the lake, turning the clear water red. His eyes glowed crimson for just a second, then glazed over. I threw the knife far into the middle of the pond and retraced my steps back to the hospital ward, where I sat again at my table and continued writing.

~

***The British Chronicle** – Friday 22nd January 1919.*

LUCKY PETE IS NOT SO LUCKY NOW

The body of Captain Peter de Ville, son of the
late Rector of St Patrick's was found this
morning, with his throat cut at the side of
a lake in the grounds of the Priory Hospital.
No weapon has yet been found.
Peter de Ville was a patient there, following
the murder of his wife and her parents
at their farm in France by a troupe of German
Soldiers. He was known in his regiment
as Lucky Pete, because of his incredible
escapes from enemy fire.
Peter de Ville leaves no known relatives.

~

Michael's following notes were obviously typed separately and were printed in hard copy format rather than added to the memory stick.

~

Notes and Comments for Suzanne

Suzanne, such a lot to happen in just two hours, the alarm did in fact rouse me from the MMM state, thank goodness.

You know my recall is accurate and I swear that the contents of item #3 are equally accurate. I know it seems fantastic, after all, how did Peter de Ville continue writing his notes if he had committed suicide by cutting his own throat? Did he, in fact, cut his own throat? Did he murder the Man in Black by the Lake or did the Man in Black perhaps murder Peter? Or was the whole thing merely his dream?

I now feel certain that through my Magic Memory Mode, I am having regressions into a previous life and these experiences are not just very strongly realistic dreams. Or perhaps it is simply that my mind is going the same way as my body – steady breakdown!

I have much to think about now, so I typed the details straight into my computer while they are still clear in my mind. Then I printed it and added my notes to the previous ones in the box that will eventually be passed to you, hopefully by me but very probably not. I intend to try and impress upon you the importance of this strange thing that is happening to me. No, I don't mean the DD (dratted disease) I am talking about the regressions that seem to begin whenever I am alone and totally relaxed. During those times, I seem to inevitably think about what has been happening to me when I am in the MMM state. Particularly where the Man in Black is concerned. There, I can type it without anything happening. I was scared it would throw me into one of the trance states, but perhaps I must be in a relaxed position to bring it about. Self-hypnosis perhaps. Dr Jennings! Now I think about that time and that person, the more I can envisage a resemblance between him and the 'M in B.'

However, Suzanne, if we do not manage to talk face to face you will receive the box and its contents on my death. I would so dearly love to see you again, my dear one.

I carefully conceal the evidence of my occupation from the prying eyes of Helena Rose and must hasten to prepare myself a cup of tea. When she arrives home, I will be reclining in a deck chair with the paper covering my face. I shall hear her of course but have decided not to acknowledge her presence. This is calculated to discomfit her and is invariably successful. She will probably pay a visit to you, poor Suzanne, this evening, for a whinge. When she is on her way home again, please phone me and I shall be able to give dear Helena Rose the impression that I can read her mind with the ease of perusing a book. Stupid woman!

~

Another page of notes apparently typed later followed here.

~

Three or four days passed before I felt inclined to transition into the next MMM session. So, having settled down comfortably with a cup of coffee close to hand, I prepared to learn more of my past existence.

I begin to suspect that the regressions do apply to me in previous lives, and after experiencing the following one I have become seriously perturbed. However, I somehow don't think I shall be allowed to stop the gentle stream from becoming a fast-flowing river.

He is always there too. The psychiatrist, known to me as Dr Jennings, whom I had chosen to nickname Dracula. Not entirely inappropriate either, as now I am convinced that he was undoubtedly Peter de Ville's 'Man in Black.'

I just must relax on my bed, think of Magic Memory Mode experiences and one…two…three…the trance is accomplished with implacable ease…I find this rather confusing. How am I able to drift off into a past existence? Is the situation in which I appear to be involved happening in a parallel universe, or is there a part of my brain that holds the memories? Or can it be that I am able to Astral-Project? No! Not that I think! Perhaps I am suffering from some sort of mental schizophrenia, which, due to my impaired movement, can only occur in my head. Whatever the reason, my recall of each session is far above that when awakening from dreams, which although I can invariably remember most of them, the details fade very quickly.

Although I can remember dreams, I certainly cannot recall any emotions connected with them whatsoever. This is not the case insofar as my MMM regressions are concerned.

The next persona is not nice, Suzanne – yet I fear he is me as I was at that time.

Please play the next memory stick #4.

~

Suzanne's Research

At this point, I felt more research was necessary if only to prove there was some substance to Michael's MMM.

I started off tracking down the British Chronicle, which it turned out had closed in 1922. It had been a private family-owned business and when Timothy Tranter died, his daughter and only living family member sold it to a magazine entrepreneur. Unfortunately, the magazine failed within a year and the property was ultimately demolished during the Second World War.

My next step was to visit St Patrick's, so I telephoned the vicar to make an appointment to meet. I arrived the next morning just before ten o'clock, our appointed time, where I discovered a charming old church with a tower rather than a spire. A path led from the vestry door through the graveyard, between a pair of huge old yew trees to a solid-looking Rectory. It could have appeared grey and forlorn, but far from it. Trees had, in an earlier age been removed and the house was set in open grounds with swathes of green lawns edged with flowers. To one side was a large pond, water lilies and feathery green strands floating on the water, with Dragonflies and Damselflies flitting back and forth in the sparkling sun. I thought I saw a frog sunning itself on a lily pad but could not be sure as I was obliged to screw up my eyes against the brightness.

The vicar walked towards me.

"Suzanne. May I call you that?"

The Reverend Gerald Cameron was a tall man with broad shoulders and a thatch of straw-coloured hair. But it was his eyes that drew attention, they welcomed me in, and seemed to read me in a single deep look. In someone else, I would have said he undressed me with his eyes, but that was not so in this case. They were the colour of dark chocolate, unusual in someone of his colouring, and the whites were so clear that they sparkled. The vicar could not be called a handsome man, but he was certainly attractive. I had become lost in the moment and before I could answer he continued, almost without a breath.

"Please call me Gerry, everyone does. Sorry, I'm going on a bit, aren't I? My wife is always saying I should slow down. Oh, shut up Gerry!" He admonished himself. "Come on into the house. It's not what you expect, is it, when you think how old it is? But it was refurbished in the 1980s. Trees cut down, grassed and landscaped. The house was modernised inside too. We think we were lucky to get this parish, the children love it, and we hold fetes and flower shows in the grounds."

He was still chuntering on when we reached the kitchen at the back. Another wonderful view through a large window of, rolling lawns, one of which boasted a croquette court.

"Switch your engine off, Gerry."

The speaker was a petite blond, who just about reached up to his armpit, wearing shorts and a crop top in bright turquoise, the bare midriff sporting a diamond stud in her tummy button. She stuck out her hand.

"His wife, Meg," she said.

"How do you like your coffee?"

"Black please," I replied. "No sugar."

We shook hands. "I'm Suzanne."

It felt as though we had known each other all our lives as we sat on deck chairs outside on the patio. Our conversation was easy, and senses of humour ran in parallel tracks. I had not felt so comfortable in the company of other people, especially strangers, for ages. Meg and Gerry apparently had four children, the eldest was married and living in Canada and the other three at the local school. I discovered that Gerry's first wife had been killed in a multiple car accident on the Motorway, which explained the difference in the ages of the children.

"Ed's my son with Alice," Gerry told me, "Adam, Kathy and Becky are ours." He indicated Meg. They seemed to like diminutives and I fully expected to be Suzy before we parted company.

Eventually, leaving Meg to prepare lunch, I went with Gerry to his study, where he had already laid out the documents relating to St Patrick's through the centuries. At the moment, my interest was in the period at the beginning of the twentieth century and from that period I discovered that the incumbent was one Reverend John de Ville. He was a widower with two sons the elder of whom bore his father's name John and the younger was Peter. The only other information I could discover regarding the de Ville family was that the Reverend John de Ville died on the 23rd of March, 1917.

I had found enough for the time being to confirm the existence of Michael's second regression.

As if to close the session at that point in time, Meg knocked on the door and announced that lunch was ready.

"Come and get it," was the way she expressed the occasion and the delicious aromas drifting from the kitchen ensured our speedy attendance.

The fresh salmon served with cauliflower au gratin, new potatoes, tiny carrots, baby sweetcorn and asparagus, followed by crunchy, nutty ice cream, was delicious. During the course of the meal, I discovered that vegetables were provided by a local farm shop and Meg actually made the ice cream herself. When I doubted I would ever be able to make such a superb concoction, Meg offered to give me a lesson the next time I visited.

We parted like old friends and I promised that the next time I visited to gather the earlier church records for my book, I would stay for a weekend.

Gerry walked me back through the churchyard and gave me a tour of the church.

"You see the silver cross over the altar," he said, "that was the actual one the Reverend John was supposed to be holding when he was found dead there."

More confirmation!

Finally, I opened the door of my little car, started the engine and with many promises to keep in touch and visit soon, I drove back home.

~

When a couple of days later, I returned to the contents of the box it was a very different story, another of Michael's regressions into what appears to have been set in another time and place. But before I could settle to concentrate the phone rang.

"Suzy?"

I knew immediately who it was.

"Gerry! What can I do for you?"

"Well, you know you mentioned that Peter de Ville had ended up in a psychiatric hospital for the armed forces." He paused for effect. "I have managed to track it down. It's still known as The Priory Hospital and although they don't have any records dating back that far, there are stories, legends if you like, about one man who was apparently writing his memoirs. He is said to have cut his throat down by the lake and all his papers and documents disappeared – or as it is told *were taken by the ghosties*. The Priory is reputed to be haunted by, wait for it" – again he paused – "by a tall man in black with a red collar in the style of a priest's neckwear."

"What do you think, Suzy? Only rumours of course but they seem to fit your story. Did I do it right?"

I had held my peace, listening and letting thoughts run ragged around in my head, but he was right. Although what he had gleaned was only rumours, they did add some sort of further confirmation that Michael's notes certainly contained some facts.

"I owe you one, Gerry. Thanks. I'm just getting down to the next stage of the story that seems to at least start in the same area, so if Meg doesn't mind, I would very much appreciate it if you can put up with me for a weekend."

"You know you're always welcome, Suzy, just give us a ring when you're ready."

We chatted for a while about the difficulties of organising the church fete, then saying goodbye I ended the call and resumed the study of the discs and cassettes before me.

Part 3
James Cameron Nineteenth Century
Circa 1850–1865

1

Item #4

James Cameron is a rebellious young man, tall and well-built, with fair hair and ice-blue eyes. He is sitting against the wall surrounding the cemetery of St Patrick's, after the grandfather of all rows with his father, the Reverend Maurice Cameron.

~

Today is my birthday, the 4th of August 1854, and only last month did I come across a copy of the London Gazette, dated 28th March 1854, where it was reported that Queen Victoria would join with Turkey, France and Sardinia against Russia. I read with excitement and realised that was what I wanted to do with my future. Realising that I needed to choose my time to put this desire to my father, I held my peace until today, feeling that he would be more inclined to listen to me on my birthday. Meanwhile, I read all I could find with regard to the war. I learned that Turkey had declared war on Russia in October 1853, a month later, the Turkish flotilla was sunk at Sinope and on Christmas Eve Sir James Graham, who as First Lord of the Admiralty, called for the destruction of Sevastopol. In February of this year, the first troops left England, and on the 11th of March, the Baltic fleet had sailed from Portsmouth. The final bit of news I was able to ascertain was that on the 22nd of June, the British had blockaded the White Sea.

I desperately wanted to join the fighting in the Crimea and had made sure that all the information accrued was in a format to appeal to my father's precise turn of mind. However, father says he expects me to take advantage of the place I shall surely earn at Cambridge, and to ultimately enter the church, like him.

"You are my only son, James," he said in his low-pitched, pleasant voice. "I cannot allow you to go adventuring at your age, and until you reach your full maturity at twenty-one you are entirely under my jurisdiction. Let God guide you my son and remember the commandment, 'Thou shalt honour thy Father and Mother'."

That was when I really blew my top.

"Just because you're a bloody vicar doesn't mean I'm interested in being one too."

"James! Language James."

"I don't give a hang for the church, as you would know if you bothered to talk to me, your son, like a grown-up human being instead of treating me like one of your retarded parishioners."

Father was horrified at these comments and the more patronising and quieter he became the more I shouted. Finally, my vocabulary ran out and I resorted to really swearing, using words the old man had probably never heard before, certainly not directed at him.

"May God forgive you, my son," he said in a disappointed voice.

"Go to hell," I shouted at him, and left the room, slamming the door hard behind me. I left the house and made my way to the graves just outside the cemetery wall. They appealed to me; these suicides and criminals who the church considered unsuited for burial within the churchyard. Well, that doesn't matter to me. I am an unbeliever, brought up in so much of the traditional twaddle of the church that the very pomp and circumstance have long since turned me away from religion.

My father, Maurice Paul Cameron, is a good man who loves his slim, elegant wife and only son, as a reverend gentleman should. But so tied up in his church, religion and the clergy is he, that had he been more cognisant of the life I choose to live, my father might understand me better. Poor father, he firmly believes that I attend church services regularly. Indeed, I truly believe he is under the misapprehension that I am a member of the cathedral choir. In his mind, I am still a young schoolboy, prepubescent and innocent.

I understand from mother that he was thirty-one before he married her shortly after the tragic death of her parents, in a fire at their home. This meant she was left with a quite considerable fortune and there was no need to rely upon the small stipend of a mere Vicar. Her parents had not agreed to the marriage, and although over twenty-one and not requiring their permission, Margaret would not disappoint them. Instead she and my father continued to meet in secret. They had been 'walking out' in this manner for about six years, and I am pretty certain that both would have been virgins at the time of their marriage. Not, of course, that any such thing would ever have been discussed with me, or anyone else for that matter.

Father refused to have Halfway Manor rebuilt, and although his marriage gave him control of his wife's fortune, he would agree only to use it for my benefit. This, of course, meant primarily my education, but as I grew older, I found I was able to cajole whatever I wanted from him. When he would not agree to my request, I only needed to approach my mother to ensure his compliance. Which just goes to show what a boring 'good' person my father is, and why he has no conception of the modern age.

~

I entered what my father would refer to as, *A state of maturity*, at the age of fourteen, with one of the maids who broke in my cherry in the stable block. Gladys was a year older than me and had considerable experience by that time. For the next year, she taught me how to copulate, holding back my ejaculation until I almost burst. I didn't manage that the first few times of course, but I did improve and by the time Gladys found herself to be pregnant, I was getting to be a pretty good stud. She had the cheek to think she could name me as the father of her bye-blow, which was not at all in accordance with my scheme of things. Before the pregnancy became evident, Gladys apparently ran away, leaving no indication as to where or why.

I knew where she was, though.

~

I have always been a loner, not mixing well at school or playing team sports. This was put down to the fact that I was, and am, extremely bright. I have always been way ahead of my peers numerically, and read many different books, from Shakespeare to Dickens, to so-called trash novels and magazines. In between, I read avidly, travel books, which is what probably edged me towards a desire to see the world.

But I digress.

There was a break after Gladys of about six months when it became necessary to employ my own hand whilst gazing at the beauties in a certain magazine I had acquired. However, I found that unsatisfying, and it was at the age of sixteen I first paid a prostitute in the city to indulge my urges.

I never used the same prostitute on a regular basis, choosing to vary my experiences, and it was thus that I learned that some women actually like to be dominated, rather than treated gently. This I found greatly increased my own pleasure – that being pre-eminent in all I do.

It was in this manner I came to meet Janice. She was a girl of my own age and had only recently decided to join the oldest profession in the world. She came from a small village in South Yorkshire and not wishing to become a drudge in some big house, had made her way to the Midlands, thinking it might improve her chances to move to a large town where she could perhaps find employment in a clothes shop. She found lodgings when she spoke to a woman in the street, who said her name was Moira. Moira immediately befriended her, promising to find her very well-paid employment, and led Janice to her own lodging house. There she introduced her to the landlady, to whom she referred as Madam Anne. Madam seemed pleased to be of help to the petite and pretty blond and allotted her a room on the same floor as Moira, instructing her to make sure Janice was made aware of the house rules.

It was by chance I came across Moira one Friday night and it was she who first introduced me to threesome sex, involving herself and the young Janice. I cannot say I did not enjoy the experience but was much taken with Janice and determined to meet with her alone (and free of charge) on another occasion. This chance occurred three weeks later. She had by then learnt the house rules and was able to entertain alone in her room. In the beginning, I was considerate of her, and she seemed to appreciate it. Then I roughed her up a little, not too much. Not enough to bruise. This only appeared to encourage her and I made a date to meet with her privately the next Sunday, entreating her not to speak of it to anyone, as they would be sure to prevent us from the meeting.

I met her by arrangement on the outskirts of town at 10.30, and we walked to the Mendip Hills, where we picnicked from the basket I had brought with me, having found a secluded place in which to rest. I made much of Janice, complimenting upon shining gold locks, and the delightful way in which the pretty dress caressed her perfect body. Then, having ascertained that she had not mentioned our assignation declared that I would love her unto death. This appeared to please her considerably and in the sheltered wooded area we shed our clothing, and I proceeded to explore Janice in a way I had not done before. The experience must have been a new one for her as well, and after a while her squeals became screams. Well, naturally I was obliged to smother those screams or I would not be able to enjoy myself to the full, so I ceased my various explorations. I needed my probing fingers to cover the no longer attractive Cupid's bow, and to grasp around her pulsing throat. By the time I had reached personal satisfaction, Janice was lying perfectly still and remained so as I removed my hands from her swan-like neck.

From that moment, I could cease to love her.

I do try never to break my word to a lady.

How ugly she looked now, tongue protruding, eyes rolled back and indications of her struggle, variously about her body. I withdrew speedily, averting my eyes. I then carefully bathed the scratches on my back in a nearby stream, having of course ensured my face was well clear of her clawing fingers during our sexual acrobatics. Then I dressed with my usual care and repacked the picnic basket, ensuring that not one scrap of rubbish was left.

I scraped a shallow grave and lining it carefully with her clothes, laid Janice reverently upon them, and having said the appropriate prayers for a burial, which, of course, I know by heart, covered her with soil. With a great deal of inconvenience to myself, I lugged large rocks and stones placing them on the grave, thus completely disguising it.

I always do a thorough job, whatever it may be.

I later asked Moira if we might arrange another threesome with herself and Janice, and was very surprised and disappointed to learn that she had moved on. Moira thought she had probably returned home to Yorkshire.

I was very careful for the next year, not allowing myself any rough behaviour, and concentrating on passing my exams for entry to Cambridge.

And so I have reached my eighteenth birthday and argued with my father. Which brings us up to date I believe.

2

Suddenly, I was engulfed by a dark shadow. I looked up from my reverie to see the tall figure of a man of indeterminate age…

"Good afternoon, young man."

His voice was a mellifluous baritone, instantly drawing me to him.

I replied, "Good afternoon sir, I am James Cameron, please join me." I patted the ground beside me.

"Thank you."

He appeared to fold himself, knees, hips, waist, like an image made of black paper. As he sat, his head now level with my own, I could see he was in fact dressed all in black, broken only by a crimson cravat, as though his throat had been cut and blood gushed under the lapels of his jacket. His face served only to complete the illusion, so pale was he, only the dark flashing eyes offering any relief beneath bushy black brows. His hair was also black, combed flat to his head from a prominent widow's peak, low on his forehead.

We observed each other for what seemed five minutes, but what was probably five seconds, then he spoke.

"I know who you are. In fact, I probably know more about you than most people, certainly more than your parents."

"W-what do you mean," I stuttered, considerably flummoxed.

"Gladys? Janice? Need I say more? I could name others who are too frightened to speak out against you."

"I don't know what you're talking about. I'm the vicar's son, for goodness' sake."

"The son of the poor vicar you may be, James, but where you are concerned, it is hardly for the sake of goodness."

I started to defend myself but was stopped as he stared into my eyes. His optics seemed to glow red and I felt myself engulfed, drawn into his hypnotic control with the loss of my own. I was silent, compliant to his will.

"Now young man, you will return to your father, apologise for your behaviour of this afternoon and prepare yourself to take up your place at Cambridge University. To all intents and purposes, you will do exactly what your father expects of you but actually, your life will take a completely different course. Your life is now in my complete control, and should you think to do other than what I prescribe, never forget I have evidence that would undoubtedly have you hanged."

I blanched, realising that this man, whoever he may be, surely knew what had happened to Gladys and Janice and probably was also aware of where their bodies now lay.

"Have no concern about that."

It seems he not only knows of my behaviour but can also read my mind.

"As I said, so long as you obey my orders for the next few years you have nothing to worry about. On the contrary, you will find I am very much on your side, and far from stopping your innovative inclinations, they will continue and indeed, increase."

"You mean you won't divulge this information to anyone and I can still…" I hesitated, "still go with women?"

"Of course, whatever you want I will encourage you to do. Just so long as when I require it, you will immediately cease what you are doing and obey me when I call. Never fear." His hand circulated in a clockwise direction. "You will know when the time is right."

Smiling, he rose to his feet and I followed suit, as though attached to him by a magnet.

"A different character from yourself may choose to ignore my call, causing the death of those whom he believes loves in most unpleasant circumstances and himself poor fellow…found by the lake of a mental asylum, with his throat cut. But that is far beyond your comprehension at the moment. Does the name de Ville mean anything to you?"

Seeing my fear he waved his long-fingered hand at me in a negating manner.

"Oh, have no fears James, my little anecdote could not possibly refer to yourself, after all, you are already one of my disciples, are you not?"

So saying, the man in black stepped away from me, into the sunlight, and by the time I had raised my hand to protect my eyes from the glare, he had disappeared. I should have been able to see him striding down the road, but no sign of him remained, it was as though he had suddenly become invisible.

I had much about which to think but decided that discretion being the better part of valour I had better find my father before doing anything else.

Having made my peace with him I asked if he knew the name de Ville. I was surprised to learn that it was my mother's maiden name. I had never known my maternal grandparents, as they died before I was born, and in all honesty, I have never evinced any interest in my mother's childhood. At least, not before I met the man in black. On that thought, I was determined to ensure that I did not offend that gentleman. Anyway, he had promised me what I desired, so putting the matter to rest in my mind, I promptly forgot about it.

~

I had set the alarm clock to wake me after two hours, at 12.30pm. Sometimes Helena Rose comes home at lunchtime, and I certainly did not want her to find me in what I now begin to realise is some sort of self-hypnotic trance. I seriously considered having a good old row with her, so she'd push off to howl on Suzanne's shoulder for a few hours but decided to hold my peace.

I was going nowhere and decided to update my computer notes during the afternoon. Besides, I was feeling very apprehensive. James Cameron's Man in Black had referred to a de Ville. Did he mean Peter de Ville whose life and experiences I have already encountered? It was now obvious that I was regressing further back, each time I, for want of a better expression, 'spaced out.' Meanwhile, the Man in Black appeared to have read the complete book, not an advantage I have so far, enabling him to envisage forward as well as back. Things would be a great deal easier if I were on the same time wavelength, but this for me is a regression by instalments.

Added A Month Later:

Unfortunately, the next morning I went down with a rotten case of influenza. Heaven only knows how I picked up the virus. I never go anywhere. I suppose Helena Rose must have brought it home – I hope she gets it too. Real badly!

That wish was granted. I should have given the situation more thought. She's at home feeling sorry for herself. I know just how she feels I had the bloody thing first, and much worse than she did. It means that I have to pretend to feel sympathetic, make her cups of tea and prepare my own food. What is more, I am unable to make any progress into what I now think of as my previous life as

James Cameron and am impatient to discover what the nineteenth century me gets up to next. If the teenage part of James' life is anything to go by, I can't imagine what lies in store during his maturity.

However, it was a full four weeks before I could do this, but I was not disappointed. Oh no! I was quite the lad in the eighteen hundreds.

What happened to get me to this state in the twenty-first century, though?

~

Eventually, over a month later, at precisely 2.05 pm, I set the alarm for 4.30 pm, which would give me time to chill out before Helena Rose got home. Recumbent upon my pillows, I allowed my mind to drift into the past and found myself back at the rectory of St Patrick's…

3

Naturally, I passed the necessary examinations and was awarded my place at Cambridge University, where I was to read the History of Religion. This was I assure you, not my choice but that of my father, who thought to bow slightly towards my inclinations, whilst still undoubtedly adhering to his own. However, although I had not seen or heard from the strange man in black since that day outside the cemetery, I was still very impressed by his presence and determined to follow his directions. He would undoubtedly call me when I was needed. And meanwhile, I would miss as many lectures as possible and enjoy myself to the full. I had a deep inner cognisance that all my papers would be done with excellence and that I would have little to do with the preparation of them. How I knew was somewhat of a puzzle but deep inside I was aware of a certain outside control.

We were expected to live on campus for the first year and although I was at first somewhat discomfited by this, I felt I should go with the flow. Thus it was that I first met my roommate, Theodore Blount. He was, like me, a freshman who also felt dubious about having to share a room. However, we were drawn to one another immediately, and our friendship developed rapidly.

Theo, as he preferred to be called, was about the same height as me, but whereas I am a blond Adonis, he was a dark saturnine figure with black hair worn below his ears where it curls outwards just at the ends. In fact, I believe that I was originally drawn to him because he reminded me of the man in black. That was purely his aura though, for in no way did he resemble that person in stature, for Theo was broad of shoulders and sturdy of legs. Perhaps it was about the eyes, which were dark and deep-set, under bushy brows that meet above his nose.

My parents had insisted on seeing me settled into my room that first Wednesday, and although I was embarrassed by this and resented it enormously, I placed a pleasant smile on my face and allowed them to accompany me. After introductions to Theo, the old man, (which is how I tend to think of my father) toddled off to catch up with some of his old friends, now professors I assumed. Mother stayed, fussing around, unpacking for me, then bringing out one of her superb fruitcakes and making tea.

"Did your parents settle you in, Theodore?" she asked.

"No, Mrs Cameron, my parents live abroad. I was granted a placement at Cambridge, which I understand is comparatively unusual in the case of a foreigner."

"I'm sure it was well deserved my dear. Would you care for more cake?"

Her minimal curiosity was satisfied and the subject would now be changed.

About an hour later, my father returned and I finally managed to persuade my mother that I was comfortably settled and eventually they were on their way home. At last, I could return to our room to get properly acquainted with my new friend. He was sitting at the table with a bottle of whiskey and two glasses before him.

"Well, my friend, peace at last, eh! Please join me."

He poured two large whiskeys, adding a small amount of tonic to his glass and raising his eyebrows in question to me.

"Please, just a little."

We sat, drinking the delectable beverage down in a draft, and refilling our glasses twice more. The final filling nearly emptied the bottle, and this time we sat in a contemplative mood. I swirled the amber liquid around in my glass and we both looked up together, about to speak.

"You first," I said.

"Very well."

"My father owns a tobacco plantation in Nicaragua. He is English and my mother was born and bred in Nicaragua, the daughter of wealthy parents, who were the previous owners of Plantation Mendosa. They both died in mysterious circumstances, leaving one child, a daughter named Pandora – my mother."

"Pater was at the time, managing the plantation, and it was he who rescued and subsequently married Pandora."

"Wow! How did they die?" This was a subject that really grabbed my attention.

"Well, you may know that Voodoo is prevalent in South America, and the area in which Plantation Mendosa is situated is no exception. In fact, we have a very active group amongst our employees – largely blacks of course, but there are certain white people that get involved too. My grandparents were found impaled on hooks, hanging amongst the drying tobacco leaves. They were both hooked beneath the chin, supported by the jawbone, and one would have expected them to die very slowly and painfully. However, this could not have been the case, as there were no signs of a struggle and only a little blood. The reason for the latter could only have been due to the fact that their bodies had been drained of blood. This draining had taken place *after* the hooks were inserted; therefore suitable containers must have been used."

"It sounds like some horrific tale told by sailors. Surely this draining of blood could only have been done by a vampire, whether of the Bat variety or human."

"That my friend is why the deaths were mysterious. Anyway, the drinking of blood is part of some of the Voodoo arts. I, of course, questioned my parents about it, but they were always unwilling to discuss the subject."

"After their deaths, as I said, my mother inherited the plantation, and in fact their whole estate, which was considerable. She had always been their adored darling and was invariably enjoying parties, balls and frequently either had friends staying at Mendosa or was visiting them. Suddenly, she found herself in charge of this huge tobacco plantation, and although well-educated by the standards of that time, she was in a panic of indecision."

"It was expected that three months of mourning would take place, so life for Pandora became very quiet, and that was when *they* first approached her."

"They?"

"Bear with me, I'll get to that in due course."

Theo sipped his whiskey and dabbed the corners of his mouth in a fastidious manner.

"Pandora was in the mansion, alone except for the servants. The kitchen staff and houseboys all live out in the native village of Plantation Mendosa, with the exception of the cook and butler. Old Tom and Meg are a married couple that have served the family for many years and have their quarters off the kitchen wing for convenience."

"She did, of course, have her personal maid Matilda, an attractive young octoroon with flashing eyes and the body of a Venus. I know this because I saw a photo of her with my mother. No one knew from whence she came. She just appeared at the kitchen door one day, bedraggled, starving and apparently suffering from amnesia. Cook took her in, fed her, tidied her up and introduced her to old Tom."

"Now, just around that time, Eve, who held the position of a personal maid to Pandora, became pregnant, and it was necessary to marry her off to a suitable buck. This way she would birth and bring up her offspring in the native village until it was old enough to work in some capacity on the plantation. The mother would then be employed in household duties until she became pregnant again. In this way at Mendosa, we breed our own workers. But I digress. Old Tom thought Matilda might be a good replacement for Eve and introduced her to his mistress, who, after interviewing the girl, agreed. Thus Matilda was brought into the employ of Plantation Mendosa, as personal maid to Pandora."

"The two girls were much of an age, about eighteen years, and although mistress and maid, they became firm friends very quickly. This was a very different state of affairs from Eve, who was some seven years older than her mistress. She could not read, was barely able to write her name and was plump and religious. These two, however, were intelligent, adventurous and impulsive, but Pandora had led a very sheltered and protected life, whereas Matilda's story was considerably different. This story came to light when the girls sat together in the orchard one evening in August. Whether or not it is true I am not sure, but if it is not, then the truth has to be something similar, judging by following events."

He paused and I endured him to continue.

"Later, old chap. I'm hungry. Let's go and get some dinner and I'll tell you more some other time."

I was disappointed but did not wish to offend my new friend, so we made our way to the refectory for dinner. After an excellent meal, we were required to attend a meeting for freshmen, which continued until ten-thirty. By the time we reached our room, we were both tired out, so retired to our beds.

~

It was Sunday of the following week before we were able to speak privately again, where, sitting on the riverbank beneath the shelter of trees, Theo continued his tale.

"Matilda gradually drew my mother away from her normal pursuits and they would apparently go for long walks together on the estate. You will appreciate that not all Mendosa is given over to tobacco plants, there are of course the drying sheds and the factory where cigars are rolled. But apart from the business side, there are acres of cultivated gardens, which include a walled garden for vegetables, and on the far side of the river, which runs through the estate from east to west, a large, forested area."

"The two girls would start by sitting quietly in the gazebo, reading to each other, then they would stroll through the garden to the bridge, where they would stop and apparently study the river, talking animatedly. As soon as they were sure no one was watching, they would run across the bridge and into the woods. I learnt this information from Cole, a young Black boy, who at the age of eight was supposed to be at his lessons."

"The Blacks attended school back then?" I queried.

"My grandparents were in the forefront of thinking, so far as workers were concerned. They believed that *all* children were capable of education, a fact that was proved many times over. In fact, my own father's plant manager is a Black, and a jolly good manager he is too."

"Anyway, Cole did not enjoy academic pursuits, he was more interested in animals, birds and insects, so whenever he could get away he did so, and he frequently tracked Pandora and Matilda on their trips into the woods. The girls would follow the river to a secluded part, where it tumbled over a rockfall and into a crevice, then they removed their clothes and frolicked in the water."

Theo hesitated as though not certain whether to continue further.

"Go on, do. You can't stop now. What did they do?"

"Pandora would lay back on a grassy bank while Matilda explored her body, kissing her breasts, pleasuring her to a state of ecstasy and telling her some of the secrets of voodoo. This apparently went on for a month or so, increasing over the period until it became daily and Matilda taught Pandora many ways of pleasuring and being pleasured. Invariably Cole watched these proceedings, fascinated. He told me that towards the end certain substances were placed on Matilda's tongue, which she inserted within Pandora's mouth, causing her to plead for more. Cole did not know what the substances were, but it was quite obvious to me that they were narcotics."

"Finally, Pandora's pleas for more information regarding the voodoo practices were granted, and the two girls slipped out of the house one night when all within were sleeping. They went to the *hounfort* by the river."

"A *hounfort,* Theo, what is that?"

"It is the name given to the area in which ceremonies occur to appease the voodoo gods, such as Damballah the snake god, who is chief of the Rada. The

Rada are considered to be the good gods, whilst the Petro, under the leadership of Baron Samedi/Cimeterre or Crois (Lord of Saturday/Cemetery/Cross), are definitely the bad gods."

"Matilda placed her finger to her lips, silencing Pandora as the girls joined the throng of people surging towards a large clearing under the trees by the river. Matilda led Pandora to a quiet place on a mossy slope under a great tree, whispering to her friend to remain still and silent. The other participants appeared completely unaware of the two girls, engaging amongst themselves and finally, having settled, proceeded with the ceremonies."

"After taking certain powdered drugs, the pleasuring began. Then around them, candles were lit and Matilda left her charge. There was now no need to enjoin Pandora to be still, as under the influence of the drugs, she was practically comatose."

Theo paused. "You appreciate that this is as I heard it from Cole. I trust him to have told me truly but you must remember that he was a mere child at the time. I made it my business to learn all I could about voodoo gods because I know that type of worship goes on at Mendosa Plantation. However, Cole has always been my friend. It was he who taught me to understand the creatures of the forest – plants that can heal and those that can kill. Make up your own mind as to the veracity of my tale."

"Of course, do please go on, Theo, I can hardly wait to hear more."

"Very well."

"It turned out that Matilda was a high priestess of the group and with Pandora suitably sedated with drugs, she led her followers in the chants and dances necessary to raise forth their voodoo gods. Cole was really frightened by what was occurring now. Previously, he had watched naked girls with beautiful bodies doing what his parents did, but with more imagination. He was watching and learning. However, this voodoo was something of which he had heard spoken in whispers but never seen before."

"He was hiding in the tree, under which Pandora lay and around which pranced naked men and women, to a rhythmic, hypnotic beating of drums. He realised that if he were to be caught now, he would instantly be taken and made one of the undead, a zombie. So he tried to control his fearful trembling and the frenzied beating of his heart, which he was sure could be heard by the voodoo worshippers below."

"But he wasn't caught?" James couldn't withhold the question.

"Of course not! How else could he have told me about it, stupid?"

"I'm sorry, Theo, please continue."

Theo looked annoyed at the interruption and sat silently, gazing into the branches above his head, as though counting the leaves and trying to ascertain if someone hidden amongst them might be spying on him.

"Please."

He reached for the bottle of whiskey and imbibed directly from it, then licking his lips, he sighed and continued.

"Then the drumbeat increased, louder, faster. Matilda stood in the centre, arms raised above her head, hands and fingers spread. She sprang from what Cole assured me was six feet in the air, landing accurately and perfectly, with no wobble, legs splayed and forming an upstanding '*X*.' At the moment she jumped, her followers prostrated themselves on the ground, forming a circle of gleaming bodies around her."

"As her feet touched the ground Matilda shouted, so loud and clear that Cole thought that the residents of the village must surely hear her. He was not one hundred percent sure of the exact words, but thought them to be:

'Come Azorath.'

"It appeared that Matilda was calling upon the gods they worshipped, for there were other names mentioned that were almost certainly those attributed to Baron Samedi.

"Then Cole noticed what appeared to be smoke rising above a rock the size of a large dining table, which was at the side of the river and half overhanging it. As he watched fearfully, the smoke changed from grey to blue, to green and finally red. There was a flash, followed by a thunderous roar and when he opened his eyes, it was to discover that he had been blinded momentarily by the bright flash, the smoke was clearing to reveal a monstrous creature. However, he was unable to describe it accurately, as he did not regain his full sight until the ceremonies ended, but I assume it to have been one of their gods."

"Do you know what it looked like?" I felt an urge to know this.

"Not really. As I said, Cole was unable to see clearly. However, I assumed it to have been Damballah, as Cole is sure that sacrifices of a black cock and a white hen were made. These are said to be used to raise that particular god. I understand that had it been Baron Samedi, the sacrifice would have proceeded with great cruelty, and the animal used would have been badly beaten, prior to having its throat cut by the *hougan*. Other animals are cruelly dealt with, according to their type. However, when I heard what followed I was less sure."

"Anyway, Matilda led the large figure, or god, to where Pandora lay under the tree. She was offered to him and he looked down upon her for several minutes in complete silence. He ran his hands over her small pubescent breasts, then her stomach to the dark hedge that covered her pubis. Then, dripping his seed where he had touched her, he swung around and catching Matilda up in his arms, strode back towards the great rock of sacrifice at the riverside. There he laid Matilda and proceeded to penetrate her.

"Pandora could surely have not survived such an assault, for although taught the ways of man by her servant and friend, she had no experience of them. Mayhap the god realised this and chose Matilda as a more satisfying sacrificial lamb. Anyway, when he had finished with her she was offered to certain of the men, whom Cole assumed were high within the order. When they, too, were satisfied, the god retrieved a slim bladed knife and drew it down from Matilda's ribs to the pelvic bone. Then he withdrew her still-beating heart, biting into it with relish, the blood running down his chin and mingling with his body hairs in three streams.

"He punched the air. There was another flash followed by thunder, and when the smoke cleared, the god was gone, as was the body of Matilda.

"The participants seemed to return to their senses at this point, which was when Cole's sight cleared properly. They hastened to clean the site of their depravity, washing blood from the rock and brushing flattened foliage, so when they had completed their task the *hounfort* was no longer obvious. Within half an hour, all the participants had departed.

"Cole stayed in his hiding place in the tree until the trembling stopped, then descending, he tried to waken Pandora. In this he was not successful, so he covered her body with her discarded clothing and ran with all speed to fetch my father."

"Was…was she dead?" I asked.

"No my dear chap, thanks to her rather inadequate figure and the fact that the drugs of which she'd partaken had virtually put *my mother* into a coma," he emphasised, making me feel the stupidity of my question. "I imagine that was another reason why the god found Matilda more to his taste. But Pandora's body had been defiled and her head was pretty messed up too."

"'Massa Blount! Massa Blount!'"

"Cole was breathless when he reached the big house, hammering on the door of the East Wing that was occupied by my father."

"'Cole! What the hell's the matter with you, boy? It's three o'clock. If you keep that racket up, you'll wake Miss Pandora.'"

"'It's Miss Pandora, Massa. You gotta come 'longa me now. She needs help. Oh Lordy, she do so need help, Massa.'"

"'Where is she, Cole? Is she in danger?'"

"'Sure is. She do need rescuin' right soon or she gonna be in more trouble. Do please comma me now.'"

"'Let me get some clothes on and I'll be right with you.'"

"My father sped off to dress, whilst Cole danced from one foot to the other, impatiently waiting for him, and within three minutes, Blount and Cole were on their way to the woods."

"Pandora lay where Cole had left her."

"'What the hell happened here?'"

"Blount was furious and Cole cowered away, expecting to be beaten, but my father is a gracious man and believes that the Black people should be given the same rights of humanity as the white man. The difference is that they are employed to perform a job of work and his job was to oversee both the Black people and whites in his employ, with justice. When I inherit the plantation, things will change I assure you."

"'You have much to tell me about this, Cole,' he said."

"Then he wrapped my mother in his coat and carried her home, and having placed her gently on the bed, covered her with soft linen and returned to the kitchen where Cole awaited him. My father heated milk for Cole and after pouring himself a stiff drink, added a small amount to the milk before handing it to the still trembling boy. After a few sips of the milk, Cole related to my father what I have told you."

"Within three months, Pandora and my father were married, and eventually, I was born."

"You will realise that I learned the story not from my father, but from Cole himself, who was thereafter employed within the household and whose education my father took upon himself. That same Cole is now the general manager of

Plantation Mendosa, a rare situation, as you will appreciate, but typical of my parents who have little regard for the opinions of their peers."

"How do you feel about all that happened, Theo?" I asked.

"Oh! I have always maintained an interest in the occult," he replied with his twisted sardonic smile.

"Do you mean…I mean does that…Do you actually practice voodoo, like in your mother's case?"

Theo laughed.

"Of course. Ever since Cole told me what happened I have realised that the semen of the gods is in me, put there by the god himself before he took Matilda as a sacrifice. My mother was saved, not because she was unconscious and small, but she was to bear me. I have powers. Powers that enabled me to come to England, to this University. Powers in which you are to share, Jamie."

Then he spoke in a voice I remembered from the cemetery of St Patrick's…

"It has been decreed that I meet and room with you, my friend. You and I have much to accomplish together that will affect this small island country, and perhaps change its future."

~

I felt excited but also nervous. This was something I had not expected, though what my expectations were I cannot tell. I suppose I hoped that with a little help from my Man in Black, I would pass all the exams I needed, with little or no work on my part, and in the end, go my own sweet way without following my father's demands. I guess I thought I would be far away from the control of my parents, free to do as I wanted when I wished. I certainly did not expect to find myself in what looked as though it would be the direct control of the Man in Black, albeit through Theodore Blount. Who is Theo anyway? Is he the Man in Black in some other guise, or is he a disciple of that creature? I cannot think of him as a man. At that time I felt considerable fear, as one always does of the unknown.

However, Theo soon set my mind at rest and between the few lectures we made it our duty to attend, so avoiding the particular notice of the professors, we partied, drank and fornicated to our heart's content.

When required, we found the necessary papers neatly written in our own handwriting, all ready to hand to our tutors. After the first couple of these, I realised that I had to at least read what was written, for my apparent lack of understanding of what was presumably my work, nearly caught me out. Fortunately for me, at my next interview with my immediate tutor, a voice in my head instructed me with appropriate responses, so I got through what could have been a disaster. However, that same voice instructed me to know in the future, or fail by my own heedlessness.

So I started reading what had been written for me and found that the information stuck firmly in my mind in a way that I fully understood, and despite my apparent lack of interest I began to enjoy that learning process.

4

At the end of the first year at Cambridge, Theo and I took off to the European continent for a six-week break. We explored France, which had some tolerable architecture, great food and magnificent women.

In Germany, the women seemed to be much taken with exercise, but not the kind Theo and I preferred. However, nearer the Swiss border, the mountainous country was magnificent, and we were enthralled by the scenery and environment in the Hartz Mountains. The town of Hamelin intrigued us – rats and the Pied Piper who led all the children away. Goslar greatly impressed us too, with its mediaeval architecture and history of witch burning.

In Italy, we explored the churches with their impressive paintings, or rather I did, as Theo refused to enter these places of Christian worship. The food was delicious and Italian women are, in my opinion, some of the most beautiful in the world. Perhaps they are so sexy because of the restraining influence religion has upon them. I interpret it as a form of rebellion.

Spain appealed to Theo excessively, particularly the bullfights. It is strange that although I have little concern for human life, I do not care to see an animal suffer. Theo could have been a Spaniard himself with his black hair, dark eyes and dusky complexion. He was in his element and I began to feel almost jealous of his involvement in the lives of our hosts. Finally, I grew tired of his constant absences, having no idea where he went or what he did, so I bucked up courage and asked.

"Theo, we decided to travel in Europe together, but since coming to Spain I have had very little of your company. Can I not join you sometime?"

"My dear chap, I thought you were happily engaged with the Spanish ladies, stamping your feet to the accompaniment of castanets, and would not be keen to indulge in politics. But please do accompany me this evening. I think you may find the experience somewhat illuminating."

So it was that I found myself involved in that about which I had disputed with my father, prior to meeting the Man in Black and subsequently taking my place at Cambridge University. In March 1855, Tsar Nicholas (I) had died and his successor Alexander (II) had little interest in continuing the war. However, a peace conference held in Vienna between March and June 1855 collapsed when the neutralisation of the Black Sea was rejected by Russia. The city of Sevastopol was still held by Russian guns, thus preventing occupation by the allies.

Theo had established a pact with some Russian students and I found myself involved in sabotaging the alliance wherever possible. After such a long and ill-prepared campaign, their clothes and boots were worn and inadequate to face the coming winter. We stole their ammunition, food and medical supplies, making worse the shortages that were already causing great suffering. I had more fun and satisfaction in those final two weeks of our vacation than all the previous four – good though they had been.

Our six weeks' break was nearly at an end, so we had to make our way back to France and onto the ferry that would return us to Dover. Despite my overwhelming desire for adventures, I was delighted to see the white cliffs of Dover as we drew near to England once again.

5

Theo and I returned to Cambridge, where through the same previous occult assistance, we attended only enough lectures to fool the professors that we were studying as required. Our papers were similarly handed in on time and gained us good marks.

We were now expected to find lodgings as freshmen would take up the accommodation on campus. This proved relatively easy and the motherly soul in whose house we became resident soon realised that her two handsome tenants preferred to be left to their own devices. However, this did not prevent her from supplying us with many good meals and a tin containing homemade cakes was always left in our sitting room. This was a good arrangement and we were satisfied to behave ourselves within Mrs Hammet's home, with polite decorum.

In actual fact, we found our excitement and satisfaction in planning and carrying out robberies. These were no simple burglaries or the pilfering of goods from shops. Oh no! We planned and acquired considerable wealth between us by stealing funds from large financial houses.

This was achieved through a careful study of the arrangements of these establishments, such as the way in which monies were transferred to businesses throughout the City, for the payment of wages to their workers. Once we had this information, it was relatively easy to remove the money and replace it with something else of similar weight and appearance but of little or no value. I shall not at this time divulge our methods, not wishing to instruct others in our personal efficiencies.

By the end of the year, we had the tidy sum of twenty thousand pounds, a great deal of which was in gold sovereigns, together with the appellation given us by the newspapers, *The Black Shadow Gang*. That gave us great merriment, for far from being a gang, we were just two students. I must acknowledge, however, that the powers of darkness were with us all the way.

Our plan was to deliver some of these funds to the terrorists with whom we had become involved in Europe during our trip to Spain the previous year, to enable them to purchase arms.

Unfortunately, because of the weight of our cargo, too obviously heavy to carry and liable to draw unwanted attention to ourselves, we decided to purchase a yacht and sail it to Europe. This would be great fun and would doubtless lower the chance of our being apprehended at the dockside.

I say, unfortunately, because we had only the most rudimentary experience of sailing, that being on the river. So sure were we of the protection ministered to us by the black forces of the occult that we set off having given no thought to such things as life jackets or waterproof clothing. It was early October during what was referred to as, *an Indian Summer*, when we embarked aboard the *Nighthawk*, taking with us only a change of clothing. The remainder of our possessions were left at our lodgings with no indication of our intentions.

Also, although we were unaware of it, our protection, presumably supplied by or through the Man in Black, was ineffective whilst on the sea, saltwater apparently being an antidote to the power of the evil one. The outcome was that the boat we had acquired was inadequate to the English Channel in rough weather, and although it was clement enough when we started, within a couple of hours a thunderstorm blew up. At first, we were elated at the speed we achieved with the strong winds behind us but it soon reached gale-force. The waves were, I believe, some twenty feet high. Our yacht was certainly more suited to calm harbour sailing than rough seas and we, being inadequately prepared, were swept into the raging waves. The last I saw of Theo was his head above the waves, cursing the weather, the sea and the world in general.

~

The last thing I can remember is the face of the Man in Black. I thought at the time that it was the face of evil personified.

Uttering a prayer to the God of my father for his intercession on my behalf, I sank beneath the waves to join my now useless wealth.

~

Michael had typed the following notes but had, for some reason, chosen to print them out again, rather than save them to the memory stick.

~

I broke off here, awakened by the loud ring of my alarm clock. I needed to think through what I had experienced during the afternoon, and it seemed impossible that I had lived nearly three years of James Cameron's life in just two and a half hours.

I had to prepare our evening meal before Helena Rose returned from work, and it was difficult to concentrate, so I pulled a couple of pre-prepared meals from the freezer, made myself a mug of tea and sat down at the kitchen table.

I knew I was becoming more involved. Not just obsessively but in a much deeper way. I am a person who needs to be in control. The one who says what is to be done. I choose what shall be eaten, whether I shall read or sleep. It is I who decrees what my wife will do, or wear…I am in control – aren't I? Not any more apparently, after all, I am the one who has this dratted disease and is more and more confined. I can't even get up the stairs to see the condition in which Helena Rose now keeps what was in our bedroom, let alone control her clothes purchases.

DAMN! DAMN! DAMN!

I am ashamed to say that I lost my temper and stamped my foot, causing such pain to travel through my toes and up my leg to a useless groin, the intensity of which necessitated a draught of mild liquid morphine. This was prescribed at a time when I was still unwilling to allow strong substances to pass my lips, preferring to fight pain with mind over matter. That's a joke, although I used to be able to cope in those days and tucked the bottle away 'for a rainy day.'

Well, I guess it must be raining, anyway, that is temporarily better!

However, I have to confess that when in that trance state, my body is controlled, occupied perhaps, by that person whom I assume was once myself. Or maybe I am out of my own body and in that of my nemesis, which sometimes seems to be more likely.

I was, <u>am</u>, frightened. For when that ringing woke me, I felt as though I had returned to my bed from a journey to another universe, or perhaps a twilight zone. I leave behind an empty shell that just lies there awaiting the returning essence that is yours truly. The return was not like an awakening, but a physical thing. As though I returned through a time warp in space, a place I had actually occupied. If this has been strange before, it is now definitely frightening. I cannot not continue. I will shut my mind to it.

No more – please.

That voice in my head, HIS voice, telling me that indeed I will continue to have my previous lives revealed. I have no choice.

I recalled that last drowning, felt the cold water seeping through my clothing, and heard the thunder of the giant waves. I was exhausted and aching, and there was an unpleasant taste of seawater in my mouth.

And the voice of the Man in Black, "You will NOT escape."

NO MORE PLEASE!

~

I typed up the previous information for you Suzanne on the following morning, determined that it would end there, on that last word – PLEASE!

But here I am once more, about to discover the next stage, or rather the previous stage of my existence.

I have managed to put off studying the next regression into my genealogy for a couple of weeks but this dratted disease is beginning to get to me and there are times when even sitting is painful. I am compelled to continue. My time I am sure is nearly done. I trust it will be the last regression, but fear that will not be the case.

I shall print a copy of my notes to you Suzanne to keep the MMM regressions separate. Why? I don't really know but it seems the right thing to do.

I will now relax on my bed and think through the last out-of-body experiences. This will almost certainly throw me into the next session.

~

The following notes were obviously added to the previous ones at a later date but were written in Michael's spidery scrawl, once again making them difficult to transcribe.

As I relaxed, it was as though I slipped back in time. I heard Dr Jennings' voice, just as if he were in the room with me. I cannot remember what brought it on, something I said perhaps? I don't know, can't remember. It was scary but I couldn't pull back...

"Relax Michael. You have been running, relax and catch your breath. Count slowly one...two...three..."

I count to myself and feel my heartbeat slow, my breath becomes even. I feel safe now.

He takes me back through my childhood, bringing to my memory things I have deliberately blanked from my mind.

As I listened to his mellifluous voice, I cringed at the pain of birth, the shock of air after the comforting aquatic existence for the previous nine months. I felt the comfort of my mother's breast as I took milk from her...

I am a toddler and from my cot between their single beds, I in the present hear my parents in time past as they dispute.

"No Jim. I have given you three sons now and God knows I did not want a second, let alone a third. Marriage is not for your disgusting sexual gratification it is for the procreation of children. Well, now I have come to the end of child-bearing, and you will never again enter my bed."

"But my dear, you are my wife and I, your husband. I am entitled to conjugal rights and you have no right to refuse me."

I do not recall hearing more of their discussion as Jennings' voice continued to take me back through time. But I do not remember my parents ever sharing a double bed, and as soon as we moved to a larger house, they did not even share a bedroom.

Then time rushed by. It was as though I was in a time machine as scenes from my childhood passed before me, but before I could adjust, I was back in real-time. It was as though we were ending what had been a regular conversation between a doctor and his patient. However, I now know differently, somehow he has a way of getting into my head and I can't stop him. Help me, please...

~

Then the phone rang. It was you, Suzanne. You still ring me, or I phone you when I know Helena Rose is going to be out. It was like the voice of an angel soothing my pain. You are never cruel, Suzanne, although you could justly be so, *that is not your way. You told me quite honestly that there is no way you wish to meet me face to face, although I have tried to persuade you to visit me and have lunch sometime, but you are adamant. You say you will always love me but that you have a strong dislike of me that is more powerful than love. That hurts but to my way of thinking now, is reasonable. I have treated you badly and cruelly. So I guess I am a very lucky man to have retained even a small bit of your love.*

I knew at that moment that I would have to pay for my treatment of the one good woman in my life before I died and shivered in fear of that future.

We spoke for an hour or more, we always have so much to talk about, always did. When we finally said our adieus, I was exhausted, and in pain from sitting too long in one position, so I lay on the bed for a while, succumbing to sleep until nearly four o'clock. Hence it was the following morning before I got down to thinking of the past and wondering about the future again.

~

It's weird. It seems that I have only to think about regressing and I find that Dr Jennings is counting me under as previously (one, two, three) and I am back in the mind of someone else, in yet another life.

~

I am intending to use a recorder after these notes and although I have managed to type and save on memory sticks so far; I think it will be necessary for me to use the recorder in the future. My fingers are becoming twisted, with arthritis in the bones, psoriasis on the palms and pain that burns in shooting agony from wrist to fingertips. So until the next time, Suzanne…

~

Suzanne's Notes

I read Michael's last notes through twice, trying to make sense of them. He was obviously in great distress, both physically and mentally. Perhaps I would talk to his doctor and friend Richard some time, but I would have to find his surname from Helena Rose and am reluctant to contact her. Partly because I can't stand the woman and partly because she will, quite reasonably, want to know why I need to speak with him, and hence what was contained in the box addressed for my eyes only. It is not easy to put off a woman like HR, better to avoid her.

So I decided to start with Cambridge University and try to trace information about James Cameron through the theological college, Emmanuel. This is one of the great old colleges representing the Church of England, so I imagine that would be where James Cameron and his father before him had received their education. I would need to call for help from Gerry once again.

Meg answered.

"Hi – St Patrick's Rectory – Meg here."

The smile on her face was revealed in the cheerful, happy voice and brought a similar one to mine.

"Meg! Suzanne here! I'm afraid I want to put upon Gerry's kindness once more, do you know if he has any contacts at Emmanuel College, Cambridge?"

"That's where he trained, Suzy, but at the moment he's out visiting a sick parishioner in hospital, although I believe he likes to be in a ward of old ladies who all worship him."

She giggled. "For goodness' sake, don't tell him I said that the bit about worshipping him I mean, goes against the grain with him, worship is for God, etc."

I assured her I would not drop her in it and after more girlish giggles and general chatter, Meg said she would ask her beloved to ring me, rather than give him a garbled message that would probably make a phone call necessary anyway.

We said our goodbyes and hung up. How long had I known these two delightful people, it seemed like all my life – diminutive Suzy and all!

Gerry called back later and confirmed he knew the Master at Emmanuel College and would arrange for me to meet with him. He would advise the Master that I was writing a book and hoped to check back on some students who had attended Emmanuel College during the end of the nineteenth century. That would ensure time saving and give him an idea of my requirements.

The following evening elicited another phone call from Gerry to confirm that he had arranged for me to visit the Master, Roland Byatt, on Friday of the following week at 9.30 am.

"You're bound to need more info after that visit Suzy," he said, "why don't you come over to St Pat's for the weekend? Meg insists and is threatening to deprive me of dinner (which incidentally smells wonderful) if I don't persuade you."

I felt a warmth of friendship, that I had thought no longer existed.

"Tell Meg I couldn't possibly be held responsible for your possible malnutrition, I'm sure you need all the energy you can get with all that rushing around the parish. Thank you both, I'll see you Friday. I can't say what time I'll get there but I am sure to be absolutely starving."

I had a week to get my notes in order and spent time going over James Cameron's life. Gerry was right, I had a visit to make to the Mendips, but where?

~

The neoclassical facade looked welcoming and the interior was no less so. A calm peace permeated the very floors and fittings and the receptionist greeted me with a cheerful smile and an invitation to sit. I did so, feeling strangely nervous, telling myself *you're a journalist for goodness' sake*, sitting on the edge of my chair leafing through the brochure about Ridley Hall. I need not have worried though, for after only about five minutes a man waddled towards me holding out a small smooth hand.

"Roland Byatt, so pleased to meet you, may I call you Suzanne? You can call me Master."

He grinned, his whole cheery face lighting up, the rosy pouches beneath his chin shaking with a glee of their own. This man could have been anything between fifty and seventy, with a veritable thatch of thick black hair and smooth skin. He is obviously a man who considers his appearance, for the hair was severely flattened by, I presume gel, and I imagine both the hair and shave to have been perfected by a professional. The clothes too, a neat navy pinstripe suit had been tailored to fit his rotund figure.

"Only joking," he continued, "it's Roland to my friends and I'm sure we shall indeed be friends. I won't tell you how my students refer to me, although knowing young Gerry I suspect he has already imparted that nickname."

He had – they call him, quite aptly I thought, Roly-Poly. However, I kept my thoughts to myself and extended my hand to shake with him. His grip was unexpectedly firm, confirming to my mind that this man was much more than the figure he presented.

"Come on, young Suzanne, let's go up to my study. Irene," he yelled to the receptionist, "arrange to have coffee and something or other to eat, sent up for me will you, dear?"

"Certainly, Master," she replied. "Doughnuts, or biscuits?"

He looked at me, shook his head, then made up his mind and said, "Both."

The study, like the man, was immaculate, three old leather-bound ledgers laid out side by side, as though set there by strict measurement. When the coffee arrived, Roland had it placed on a coffee table before two buttoned burgundy leather club chairs and invited me to sit. The coffee was good and I managed one chocolate biscuit at the Master's insistence. He ate two sticky looking iced doughnuts and added a dash of brandy to his coffee. I declined his offer.

Finally, we got to discuss the reason for my visit.

Donning cotton gloves, a process which, of course, was totally appropriate, and which was a process that I was sure the Master would never ignore, he opened the yearbook for 1815. Maurice Paul Cameron had been a freshman that year and proved to be an exemplary student, graduating with an honours degree four years later. It was noted that he was a missionary in the jungles of Brazil for the next five years. On his return, he had entered a retreat in Hampshire for a period of six months. For the next eighteen months, Maurice Cameron had covered various parishes before being offered the Parish of St Patrick's in 1828. He eventually married one Margaret de Ville in 1830 and six years later, James was born.

James Cameron, Maurice's son, entered his father's old college at the tender age of fifteen. He apparently passed all the necessary examinations and undoubtedly arrived at the university in September 1854, when he moved into shared accommodation with one Theodore Blount. There was no further record of his having spent time at Emmanuel. Neither boy appears to have attended any lectures and produced only a few papers, all of which were satisfactory and indeed above average. Their lodgings, the rent having been paid to the end of the year, was then cleared and left for the use of other students.

"What would have happened to their things – clothes, books?" I asked.

"They would have been returned to their parents, as appropriate I imagine. Said parents would have received a letter asking them to collect the property of their respective sons. I presume James's mother and father and Theodore's father had no idea at the time, that the boys had disappeared."

"I agree with you there, they must have been receiving periodic letters or they would surely have contacted the University. So there's nothing else you can tell me about James Cameron?"

"Hmm!" The Master's cheery face was serious now his mouth downturned, looking more like an unhappy bulldog.

"I would appreciate it if you feel able to tell me a little more about the book you are writing."

We silently looked at each other for what seemed a long time as I made my decision to trust this man. Then I removed the papers I had written about James Cameron, without troubling to make any explanation, and passed them to Roland Byatt to read. He proved to be extremely perspicacious.

"So," he said, "this is a regression. But not a novel. These weird experiences are or were actually happening to someone you know."

"Yes, my late ex-husband. He asked me to look into what was happening to him after his death. He was dying when they started and he didn't want his second wife to know about them, so he left me a box of recordings, memory sticks and some typed and written notes. I feel it is incumbent upon me to try and prove the veracity wherever possible, so here I am."

The Master rubbed his eyes.

"I'm getting dried up in here," he said. "Let's go and get some lunch at the Pub."

We left the building and crossed St Andrew's Street into Downing Street. Passing Sedgwick Museum and the Museum of Archaeology and Anthropology on our left. Then, turning into a narrow lane that the Master informed me was known as Free School Lane, we eventually reached The Eagle in Benet Street. Sitting in the garden of The Eagle with its cobbled courtyard, I felt more relaxed than for a long time. The lunch was a superb steak and kidney pie that Roland assured me was made in the kitchen of the pub, served with fresh local vegetables. I settled for a coffee but Roland said he believed a meal was not complete without apple pie and ice cream to complete it. I felt I needed the coffee, black and more than one cup when I realised that we had finished the bottle of Burgundy between us. I had a long drive ahead of me.

By the time we parted, Roland knew the entire story to date and had promised to delve into the local paper archives in an endeavour to find if anything had been reported about two people being drowned at sea, whilst on board a yacht that had sunk during a storm.

It was late when I arrived at the Rectory but Meg had a slow casserole simmering and it took only half an hour to settle into the large room complete with an en suite bathroom. I quickly freshened up and changed into a loose-fitting summer dress, then descended the wide staircase and found my way to the kitchen. Gerry had set the table and Meg was stirring the rice in a pan.

"Red?" asked Gerry.

I responded, "Yes, please."

After the meal, we sat there around the kitchen table as though it was the most usual thing in the world and discussed my visit with the Master. That was the way he was always referred to between us – the Master.

Eventually, we made a move and stacked the dishwasher, then each of us clutching a mug of coffee retreated to the lounge. I had not seen this room before. It ran the whole width of the house, from side to side, the floor was parquet with a large Chinese rug at one end. A television was mounted on the wall, with two plump settees and two matching chairs covered in heavy fabrics that were perfect for the room. At the opposite end was an oak refectory table with a wheel back carver at each end and three wheel back chairs on either side, complete with a court cabinet.

Gerry had switched the overhead lights on as we entered the room, but once we were comfortably seated, he replaced them with wall lights. I had not felt so at peace in a room since my marriage had dissolved. And when we finally stopped talking, with Mozart playing quietly in the background, I'm afraid I dozed off. Meg shook me awake and suggested I retire to bed. I had the best night's sleep I can ever remember.

It was a fabulous weekend, we walked the dogs, played tennis and went to a garden fete. I shall need to diet for a week to expunge the weight I must have added after Meg's frequent and wonderful meals. I also attended the morning service at St Patrick's, something I had not done for many years but the old memories of the service soon returned. Gerry's sermon was short and to the point, and the hymns were from the old Redemption Hymnal so I knew the tunes if not the words.

It was a time of peace and contentment and by the time I left early Monday morning, I felt as though I was leaving behind my own family.

Michael has done more for me through this quest than he ever did as my husband. I think at the end he would have been pleased to know that he is the catalyst that gained me three new friends, for I do indeed feel that Meg, Gerry and the Master Roland Byatt are real friends, not just acquaintances.

Settling back into the life I knew so well actually took me a couple of days and it was not until Thursday that I forced myself to sit down and consider the next part of Michael's regression. He appeared to have entered a period during the seventeenth/eighteenth centuries. But this was different, as he appeared to be an observer/narrator of at least the first portion. There were also two diaries to which he referred. Where they came from I do not know, but their relevance definitely seems to be appropriate and I shall include them wherever they appear to fit the narrative.

Michael's narrative regarding his next regression was recorded on his handheld recorder and at times I felt it was actually spoken during his trance rather than after it. However, there were breaks where it seemed appropriate to insert entries from the diaries.

Part 4
Henri De Ville
Part I
Seventeenth/Eighteenth Centuries

1

Item #5

Father Gregory, Prior of St Patrick's Priory, stood in the doorway of the chapel silently watching. The nun had been unmoving at prayer for the past three hours and the good Prior was worried. He walked silently down the aisle, sliding along the pew beside her, gently laying his hand on the bowed head.

"Sister Teresa."

The nun jumped.

"Oh! Father Prior, you scared me half to death."

"Do you wish to talk, Sister? You have been here many hours since."

"The child, Father."

"Ah! Lady Isabella's child I presume."

The nun knuckled her eyes and straightened her wimple. Sister Teresa had been a member of the hospice attached to St Patrick's Priory for close on fifty years, having taken her vows when she was sixteen years of age. Chubby apple cheeks bulged beneath kindly blue eyes, but the full lips lacked their usual cheery smile. She shook her head, then made up her mind…

"Father, Lady Isabella swore me to silence before she died, but I do not think I am capable of dealing with this alone. I have prayed for guidance and you are my answer to prayer, for only you could possibly share this secret with me. The story is an unhappy one, with an unimaginable depth of evil that I fear involves some that are known as fellow members of the Church of God. Lady Isabella begged that the child be kept within the walls of the Priory, his education be carried out by yourself and the monks and that in due time he becomes a noviciate, thus living his whole life within the sanctity of St Patrick's Priory."

"I can see no difficulty there, Sister. The child is a boy and the priory has seen to the education of such as he, in the past."

The Prior sat in deep thought, chin resting on steepled fingers. He was a compact man with fine effete features and faded blue eyes. The grey fringe of coarse hair, cut evenly around at earlobe level, surrounded his tonsure.

"During his babyhood, you and the Sisters of Solitude will have the care of this child. As he grows, I will ensure that he receives integration with the monks, which will give him both mothers and fathers."

He looked pleased with himself, then recalled…

"The father of the child, Sister, who is the father?"

Sister Teresa clasped her hands over her mouth, as though to prevent the telling.

"Lady Isabella…the last words she whispered to me were those of his name. She was greatly afraid."

"Yes, yes, Sister, the name, what is it?"

Sister Teresa chewed on her bottom lip, then leaning towards the Prior, whispered in his ear…

"What?"

All the colour drained from his face and rising he approached the altar, over which hung the crucified Christ. Prostrating himself he prayed silently for several minutes, then rising to his knees beckoned Sister Teresa to join him. Side by side, the two elderly children of God prayed for the future soul of the child they had undertaken to educate in their midst. Finally, sitting together in the front pew, they discussed what might be undertaken for the good of the child, whom they decided should be named Henri de Ville, taking the family name of his mother.

"Is it known how Lady Isabella de Ville came to give birth at the Hospice of St Patrick's? Who brought her here?"

Sister Teresa bowed her head.

"She was brought here by her father."

"Baron Dominitus de Ville?" The Prior interjected.

"Just so. May I relate all I know, Father? It will take some time."

"Please, Sister Teresa but let us retire to my quarters. We are both in need of refreshment."

A door at the rear of the chapel led into a small, enclosed passageway, at the back of which, rose a steep stone staircase. At the top of this stood a solid oak door with metal door furniture of shining brass. The Prior withdrew a large key from his robe and inserting it in the lock opened the door to his quarters on the second of three levels, in the tower. The circular room boasted slit windows at regular intervals around its circumference. But the extra light they provided was the only difference between this cell and those of the rest of the monks of St Patrick's. A simple truckle bed, its head between two slit windows, held a thin horsehair mattress, covered by two blankets. At the side of the bed was a wooden chair and placed where the light was to best advantage was a table, with another wooden chair pushed beneath it. A Prie Deux was at the foot of the bed, its kneeler worn and the wood smoothly indented with use. A plain cupboard contained Father Gregory's robes of office and the washstand held a bowl and jug of water.

The Prior withdrew a bottle of wine, brewed at the Priory by Father Bachus and two noviciates. The clear red liquid flowed into the two glasses and Father Gregory placed bread and cheese on the board between them on the table. Sister Teresa ate very little, but colour returned to her cheeks as she sipped the wine. With a sigh, she began her story…

"As you are aware, Father," she said, "there is only one patient at the hospice, old Grundy the tramp. So when Lady Isabella was brought in late the night before last, I was the only one on duty."

She paused again, gathering together her scattered thoughts.

"It was just one o'clock. I know that for sure because as I opened the door, the tower clock struck the hour. The banging on the door was so loud that I rushed to open it before *everyone* was disturbed. If you remember Father, there was a thunderstorm on Sunday night and torrential rain. The wind almost wrenched the door from my hand and I was drenched in the few moments I stood there. The Baron was stamping his feet and was about to hammer on the door again, as I opened it" – Sister Teresa paused – "have you met Baron Dominitus, Father?"

He shook his head and Sister Teresa continued.

"I can best describe him as a big, red man. He is of about your height but with broad shoulders and wide in girth. I could not fail to notice that his stomach was somewhat larger than that of his pregnant daughter." She blushed. "I'm sorry Father, forgive my careless tongue. His face was rather purple than red, and his hair was like bushy dry grass, the colour of carrots."

"I mean no offence, Father, but describing the man may give some insight to his actions."

"I understand, Sister, pray continue."

"I invited him in and he blustered, saying, '*My daughter is in the carriage, you must take her in but I demand your silence. Her child will be smothered at birth.*' I again invited him to fetch his daughter and bring her to the warmth and comfort of St Patrick's Hospice, and after much puffing and muttering, most of which I could not hear, he turned and a while later returned, pushing the poor girl before him."

"They came in and I showed them to the office, where before I could speak Baron Dominitus flung himself into a chair with such force that I thought it would collapse under his weight; and allowing me no time to speak, shouted, '*Get Sister Margarita!*' I tried to tell him that the Mother Superior was sleeping and could not be disturbed, but he stood, and grasping my shoulder, pushed me roughly towards the door. He told me to advise her that the Baron Dominitus de Ville wished to speak with her regarding the Sisterhood of the Golden Orb."

"Oh, Father! I was frightened by that man, so I did as he bid. Mother Margarita was not pleased with me but bade me return, ensure he was given refreshments, and tell him she would be with him shortly. When she entered some ten minutes later, I was instructed to escort Lady Isabella to a room and attend her through the birthing."

"Lady Isabella was shivering with cold and fear, so I helped remove her damp clothing and put on a nightgown warmed on the bedpan I had placed in the bed after waking the Reverend Mother. Then, reassuring her of my early return, I left to prepare some chicken broth. She was sleeping when I returned and I thought it better to leave her resting, so having checked on old Grundy and finding him snoring, I took up my sewing and sat beside Lady Isabella."

"For an hour, she slept the sleep of one exhausted. Then her face and movements indicated that she was dreaming. She tossed and turned, moaning and calling for help. I tried to soothe her, wiping the perspiration from her brow with a cool, damp cloth. Her mutterings were hard to decipher, but I did hear her say, '*Golden Orb – get away – must get away.*' Then with a scream, she awoke, sitting up, her face streaming with the perspiration of her high temperature and racing pulse."

"It was difficult, Father. I had to comfort her, drawing her into my arms and allowing her to sob on my shoulder, whilst I patted and smoothed her beautiful auburn hair. Gradually she calmed. Looking embarrassed she drew away from me. I plumped up her pillows and seeing her comfortable, went to fetch some warm broth. Poor dear, she was hungry and after eating said her thanks and asked me to pray with her. Then she asked if I would hear her confession."

"Of course, I told her I could not but offered to fetch you, Father. However, she would have none of that, so I suggested that perhaps the Mother Superior would be the one to whom she should speak. At this suggestion she appeared very frightened, saying, *'Please, please, I do not ever want to see her, Sister Margarita is my father's—'* I asked her what she meant, her father's what? But she replied, *'just my father's.'* Then withdrawing into herself, she said in a voice that I think I was not meant to hear, *'His and the Sisters of the Golden Orb.'* Once again, she begged me to hear her confession. Oh! Forgive me, Father. But what could I do? So I agreed, with the grace of God, to take that responsibility. However, I did manage to get her agreement that if she did not survive the birth, I could, at my own discretion, repeat her confession as part of my own, to my confessor. She, of course, was unaware that within the order of the Sisters of Solitude, our confessor is Mother Superior, and I can never repeat Lady Isabella's confidence to her."

Sister Teresa looked imploringly at the Father Prior. "Would you be willing, Father, to hear my confession now?"

Making the sign of the cross Father Gregory nodded his agreement, and Sister Teresa spoke the words of the confessional.

"Bless me, Father, for I have sinned."

She looked at the good Prior. He once again made the sign of the cross, saying, "Continue sister – please."

"Father, I have been guilty of the sin of pride in that I took it upon myself to hear the confession of a young woman in extremity. I am guilty of withholding information from my Mother Superior and speaking of her to another without her permission. I wish now to relate that which I heard, just prior to the death of that person and with her permission to do so at this time."

She paused again, then pulling herself together, continued.

"When she was but twelve years of age, her father promised Lady Isabella de Ville in marriage to an older man. Lord Fitzhugh was of indeterminate age, and she said that from her point of view he could have been fifty or a hundred and fifty. Apparently, he asked Baron Dominitus for the hand of his daughter and, being a man of great wealth it was gladly given, and sealed in the usual manner, with a handshake and a glass of porter. It did not occur to the Baron to speak of this to his daughter and the first she heard of the matter was one month prior to her fifteenth birthday, when her father advised Isabella that on her birthday she was to marry Lord Fitzhugh. The poor girl was terrified. She had on several occasions met the man in her father's house and had no liking for the large, arrogant creature. His voice was loud, his nose red and bulbous and his breath foul-smelling with halitosis. Isabella begged her father to retract his promise but was firmly denied any such thing."

The nun paused, sipping her wine, deep in thought.

"Pray continue, Sister Teresa."

"I am sorry, Father. Her ladyship's mother died when her daughter was only five years of age, and she was brought up by a series of servants and governesses. Having no siblings, Isabella was a lonely child, left to her own devices for many hours at a time. This inevitably led to a close relationship with the servants, who you will appreciate, adored the beautiful child. Thus, it was her governess/companion to whom she turned for help."

"Susan Blessed had been governess to Lady Isabella since her ninth birthday. A sweet religious girl, Susan was the daughter of the late Reverend Charles Blessed. Like her charge, Susan's mother had died when her daughter was only five, so the two girls had much in common, despite a six-year age difference."

"At that time, Lady Isabella had no money of her own, although she would inherit fifty thousand pounds from her mother's estate on the occasion of her twenty-first birthday, or upon her marriage. That amount would then, of course, automatically become the property of her husband, in accordance with the law. However, Susan Blessed had saved most of her wages of twenty pounds per year since the commencement of her employment. After all, she had no relatives to support and required very little. The two girls sat on Isabella's bed and counted the money, which amounted to one hundred and sixteen pounds, three shillings and ten pence."

"They planned to walk to the Hospice run by nuns at St Patrick's Priory, and once there, to place themselves at the mercy of Mother Superior. Lady Isabella and Susan Blessed were both willing to take the veil in order to escape the marriage to Lord Fitzhugh."

Sister Teresa bowed her head, shoulders shaking once more as she wept for the very sorrow of the situation.

Father Gregory patted her shoulder and bade her take more wine, saying, "There, there, Sister. Please do not upset yourself so."

"They…they came to St Patrick's Father. For sanctuary."

The Prior's eyes widened, brow raising and cheeks flushing.

"But I knew nothing of this, Sister. Surely Mother Superior would consult me on this matter?"

"It happened some five years ago and at that time I was in recluse at the Arlington Retreat. But yes, the Reverend Mother should have consulted you as the Prior. Lady Isabella said that Sister Madeleine opened the Hospice door to them and escorted them directly to Mother Superior. They were given food and taken to a room where they could sleep. The two young women stayed within the confines of the Hospice for three weeks, and during that time were served by only Sister Madeleine. They saw no one else, apart from Mother Superior."

"At the beginning of the third week, she sent for them and explained that it had been arranged for them to travel to the convent of the Sisters of the Golden Orb. Once there, they would become noviciates within the closed order. However, before leaving, the Reverend Mother required their signed acceptance of the fact that for the rest of their lives, the two young women would be confined within the estate of the Convent of the Golden Orb. Lady Isabella, in fear of her father, signed gladly but her companion, Susan Blessed, asked for time to consider. She was granted time until after vespers, and in that period Lady Isabella had persuaded her that it was the best thing to escape to Switzerland. She also told Susan that she was certain there would be a time of grace when if she did not feel suited to the life of a nun, she would be able to withdraw. So it was that at the end of the week the two were despatched by coach to Harwich, where they boarded a ferry to carry them across the Channel. Sister Madeleine accompanied them throughout this journey."

The Convent of the Golden Orb proved to be high in the mountains of Switzerland, being completely isolated, and in the winter cut off from main roads by snow and ice. Lady Isabella said that the convent is built partly into the mountain peak and that there is a circular clearing, giving an unimpeded view of anyone who is on any part of that area leading to the convent. At the base of the mountain slope, and completely surrounding the mountain, is a pine-forested area, being dark, close and of about one mile in depth. This forest is enclosed within a high stonewall, topped with broken glass and there is apparently only one entrance to the convent, guarded by a wooden gate, bound by iron supports. This is kept locked at all times and access or egress can only be obtained when opened by the chief groundsman, who lives in a cottage just inside the gate with his wife and sons. He, in turn, always relies on permission from the Mother Superior."

"How would he obtain that, Sister, being some three miles from the convent?"

"I too asked that question, Father. Lady Isabella said it was achieved by a series of flags. Normally, a black flag with a golden orb is flown from the tower. If she wished to allow egress, Mother Superior had this withdrawn and a bright red flag was erected in its stead. The groundsman, in turn, would advise if someone wished entrance to the convent by sending one of his sons running the three miles to the door of the convent. Upon which, if Mother Superior allowed it, she would have someone raise the red flag. It seems a bit complicated, doesn't it? Surely the groundsman's boy could run down again with the answer, but anyway I imagine visitors were few and far between."

"Indeed. Yes. The two young women were there for how long? Do you know this?"

"Yes, Father, but it is a long and complicated story and I fear I am finding it difficult to recollect clearly."

"My fault, Sister Teresa. My fault entirely. I have been so engrossed by your tale that time has no meaning. It is late and I fear it is nearly time for the vespers bell to ring. Under the circumstances, the Lord God will no doubt forgive our sin of neglect. Go, Sister. Go back to your charge, for the baby boy needs to know the woman who will raise him, as his mother would have done. We must talk more of this though, for I would hear all of the Lady Isabella's experiences if we are to carry out her wishes."

~

The Vespers Bell…

It took me a moment to readapt to the present, to realise that the bell I could hear was the telephone. After seven rings, the machine clocked in with my voice reverberating on the telephone's speaker…DEVILLE SPEAKS…LEAVE A MESSAGE IF YOU WISH BUT ENSURE IT IS COHERENT AND ACCURATE…

Suzanne's voice could be heard, "Michael? Michael, please pick up the phone."

I did so, setting the recorder. "I am here Suzanne honey, to what do I owe this pleasure?"

"Helena Rose came to my house last night. She says you are getting worse, Michael."

"A little maybe, but as you can hear I am in full control."

"It's not that. Not just that."

(She is hesitating, trying to tell me something difficult to say. Damn! I have enough on my mind without her trying to mother me, or whatever).

"In the past HR..." *(Suzanne is the only one with whom I indulge abbreviations of names, and anyway she usually refuses to speak of my second wife by the name I chose for her. Thus I accept the diminutive of HR).*

"In the past, HR has only visited me when you two have quarrelled. She uses me as a sounding board because I've experienced the same things, more or less. But last night she kept telling me how unwell you are, how much worse. She said you can no longer manage to get around to prepare a meal or even make tea. In fact, she says that you can only just manage to feed yourself and struggle to the toilet. Is that right, Michael?"

"No, it's not entirely right. I confess I am weaker now and have to rest more frequently. I can still shower and dress, but I do tend to wear sweatshirts or polo shirts if it's hot – things that just slip over my head. I don't always bother to zip my trousers either and socks have been replaced with boot-slippers. I don't like to discuss this though, so I have said it once only, to set your mind at rest. I also confess that I do make excuses to HR so that I no longer feel obliged to prepare our meals. She can do it when she gets home from work."

"That sounds like the Michael I know, love and dislike. Do you really hate her so much?"

"She is unkind to me, Suzanne, not something you could nail down, but by omission."

"Be careful, Mike. HR hates you too. She wants you out of her life so she has full control of your house and money. I'm afraid you might have a sudden heart attack or an accident. Maybe even commit suicide, like she tried to encourage me to do before I left you. Remember, she is capable of it and knows her poisons, so take care."

"I will, I promise."

"I've just decided on the spur of the moment to tell you that I am putting down something that might interest you, to ensure that you realise that what I *have said or written is true, not imaginary however much they might appear to be so. Please promise to read them thoroughly, and after my demise to decide what should be done with them. You know me better than most. No, better than anyone else in the world. You know I am absolutely serious."*

"I willingly give my promise, asking only that you pass what you have already written to me as soon as possible, for safekeeping."

(I promised to do so but was determined in my mind to complete this quest into my past first).

"Goodbye, Suzanne."

"Bye Mike."

~

The recording had finished here and Michael continued his narrative later.

~

That short conversation had made my day, so I hobbled to the kitchen to make scrambled eggs and toast, determined to ensure I ate nothing prepared by my wife/nurse in the future. I then transferred all my medications from the bathroom cabinet to my bedside set of drawers. I will attend to my own taking of tablets henceforth and insist upon bottled water instead of that from the tap placed by my side in a jug by my wife.

Helena Rose was full of kindly concern upon her return that evening, worried as to my health when I refused dinner. I instructed her to go out and purchase bottled water, saying I'd heard something on the radio that indicated tap water was not recommended for one suffering from my particular disease. I adopted my loud fierce – do as you are told or else – voice so that she was too scared to refuse the order. She returned about half an hour later, during which time I had retired to my bed.

"Shall I open a bottle for you, darling?"

She spoke in that whining voice she fondly thinks of as a concerned, caring one. But I refused, saying I didn't want any now, but when she left, I pulled the gripper from under my pillow and opened one myself. I need to phone Suzanne tomorrow and get her to bring me some supplies of biscuits and other nibbles, to tide me over without Helena Rose realising what precautions I am taking.

This is quite exciting. Now I seem to be able to slip into my past existences at will, although I do perhaps need something to drag me back to the present. Must remember to set the alarm each time. In my last regression, it would appear that I have just been born as Henri de Ville – a bastard, whilst in the present day, I am perhaps, looking forward to an untimely death by the hand of my wife/nurse. However, I am determined to find more about Henri's life at St Patrick's Priory.

This regression thing is getting spooky though. The first served to remind me of my encounters with the psychiatrist Jennings and it is as though he is the catalyst. The Man in Black perhaps? In the previous ones, I was Peter de Ville and James Cameron, taking part in what happened in their lives, but this time it is more like watching a film. I am there but remain completely unseen. I see and hear the old Prior and Sister Teresa talking about Henri, who I am certain will be revealed in later life as a pre-existing me! I am allowed to hear of my mother's misfortunes, and I imagine that story is only half told so far. Sister Teresa has much to still convey to Prior Gregory and I want to make sure I do not miss any part thereof.

I slept well that night and was woken by Helena Rose bringing me a cup of tea and toast. I muttered to leave it on the bedside cabinet, which she did. Then, kissing me on the brow, she departed for work. I heard the jeep start and drive off then struggled to a sitting position and swung my legs gingerly over the edge of the bed. I didn't feel too bad this morning, but it always takes about an hour to truly limber up.

Eventually, I ditched the tea down the drain and toast into the bin. I must remember to tie the bag up for her to put in the wheelie. Don't want her to go through the contents, do I? Made coffee and cereal, ate it, and forty minutes later picked up the phone. Since leaving me, Suzanne has taken up freelance journalism, mainly, I believe, with a magazine, which is proving to be very successful. It also has the advantage of allowing her to work from home a lot of the time. I metaphorically crossed my fingers (a total impossibility now) that she would be home and depressed the button programmed to Suzanne's number. She must have been close by because the phone was picked up almost immediately. I told her of my decision about Helena Rose and food, gave her a shopping list and promised to exchange the things she bought for cash.

~

I am now the unseen presence.

Does that mean I am a ghost – a spirit – an essence of whom I would become?

Why am I being allowed to see what happened before my birth as Henri de Ville? No doubt all will be revealed in good time.

So I relax in the recliner, ready to find out more about my past. The doorbell would get through to me…I hope…

2

They were back in the Prior's room at the top of the tower, sun streaming through the southern window slits, dust motes dancing in the slides of light and warming the stone floor where it landed. The old nun and Prior sat on either side of a solid wooden table, mugs of milk before them.

~

It was as though they had been waiting for me to arrive.

~

"I have thought much about the rest of this tale, Father, and feel unable to repeat what I know, what I have learnt from reading the diaries of both Lady Isabella de Ville and Susan Blessed."

"Ah! So the ladies kept diaries, did they?"

"Yes Father, she bade me remove the two books from her reticule whilst we were speaking. In fact, it seems that they both did so more or less regularly after their arrival at the Convent of the Golden Orb. To get the whole picture it is necessary to peruse the writings of the two young ladies."

"During her time at the Convent of the Golden Orb, Isabella saw Susan for the first week. From that time, they were separated and given no opportunity to see or speak with each other. And those circumstances prevailed for the next nine months, after which everything changed dramatically."

"I feel you will understand better what happened by reading rather than listening to my retelling the story, so I will, if I may, leave the two diaries with you. Personally, I read first Lady Isabella's then Susan's, but you may find it more comprehensible if you were to read them side by side, day by day.

Remember, at the Convent of the Golden Orb the two friends were separated, therefore some of what they have written is almost like hearing a conversation."

"Thank you, Sister Teresa. Go about your business and I will send for you when I have finished. But stay! The baby Henri, how fares he?"

"A beautiful boy, Father, healthy and a joy to behold. And so bright, I do believe that the baby child understands everything around him."

"And I do believe that your heart has been stolen, Sister Teresa. With God's help, the child will develop without the influence of his evil papa."

Sister Teresa bowed her head, making the sign of the cross and saying "Amen," left the room.

Leaning his elbows on the table, Father Gregory opened the two diaries. One, that of Lady Isabella, was a fine book about half an inch thick and bound in burgundy leather, tooled with gold spirals. Her writing was a neat script in a large, almost childish hand. The other was about the same thickness but consisted of sheets of paper between two mismatched pieces of board that had been stitched and tied with wool. This was nevertheless neatly done, presumably by Susan, whose writing was a tight script that was kept sparingly small. Setting them side by side as suggested, the Prior commenced reading. He soon discovered, however, that as the diaries appeared to be undated and sometimes were apparently not sequential, it would perhaps be up to him to try and decipher what might turn out to be somewhat of a riddle.

~

It was here that Michael inserted one of his handwritten comments.

I read the diaries alongside or over the shoulder of Prior Gregory but as you will notice the writings amongst these notes are as handwritten by the two ladies. Bear with me, I will explain later.

~

Lady Isabella's Diary – Switzerland

This afternoon I was called to Mother Superior's office. This perturbed me, as such an order was generally only issued for a very serious misdemeanour and I was sure no such thing had occurred. It was this occurrence that encouraged me to write daily in my diary again. I had done this since I was ten, but with the trauma of possible forced marriage and our retreat to the convent in Switzerland, has been cast to one side until now. I must have had some internal knowledge that such writings would be strongly disapproved of here because on arrival I secreted my diary under the mattress of my bed. This feeling was confirmed when Sister Aureole brought my writing case forth and informed me that no letters were permitted to be either received or sent. However, I was able to assure her that I kept it only in remembrance of my dear mother and it contained only my Bible that was once hers. I did not mention that it also contained my writing implements, and fortunately she showed no further interest, so by this deception I was allowed to keep it.

When Susan and I arrived at the Convent of the Golden Orb, it was November and was incredibly cold. Sister Aureole seems to be the one in charge and she was very kind, showing us to adjoining rooms that I later learned to refer to as cells, and bringing us a hot delicious meal that we ate in mine. For the first week, we were accompanied to attend some of the services. A choir sang Gregorian chants that were a joy to hear, and I could have spent many hours just listening to them. Susan was all of a fidget though and tried to question Sister Aureole, with little success. I feel perhaps that it was this that brought about what followed.

On the morning of the seventh day, Susan did not accompany me to morning prayers and when I asked Sister Aureole where my friend was, she responded that it was considered our training as noviciates would be best accomplished in separate wings of the convent. I was to train in the West wing and Susan in the East. Knowing nothing of the working of such establishments I accepted this situation, trusting that we would meet in the refectory at mealtimes. <u>I have not seen my dear friend for seven weeks!</u>

We have been here for two months now and I have fallen into a peaceful routine of prayers, services and the other daily activities of my wing. No speaking is allowed at mealtimes but during dinner, someone reads from a religious text. Yesterday was my turn, which I enjoyed immensely. I read Chapter 5 from the book of Genesis, which gives the generations of Adam. Is it not amazing that

Adam himself lived for 930 years? In Chapter 6, God sees the evil of mankind – how sad he must have been. I would so like to discuss our daily readings with the other residents of this place but the conversation is frowned upon. I fear that without the daily readings we would lose the power of speech.

Now with my heart all-aflutter, I am today to be escorted to Mother Superior's office immediately following silent prayers, which are conducted in the small chapel.

More later.

~

On arriving at Mother Superior's office, I found her to be overly kind, which served to worry me even more, as this is not her natural form of behaviour. She gently took my arm and led me to a sofa, where she sat beside me and we prayed together. With the inevitable ritual completed, Mother Superior proceeded to advise me that Susan had, that morning, apparently fallen from a high cliff at the rear of the property. Sister Joseph had seen her fall and immediately reported the matter to Sister Marie Boudica, administrator of the convent. The groundsman had been found and with others had gone to the place from which Susan had fallen and, lying on his stomach he cautiously peered over the edge of the cliff. She told me that the drop is some two hundred metres into a widening fissure, with a fast-flowing river at the base. The only sign they could discern of the tragic fall was Susan's cloak, caught on a sharp rock about halfway down.

I am distraught, being by no means happy at the convent and already missing the companionship of my dear trusted friend of so many years. My final chance to seriously discuss with Susan a way of recanting our earlier vows is now gone. What am I to do? Surely in this place, God is present, but it appears to me that the presence in the Convent of the Golden Orb is rather that of Satan himself than that of our Lord. Nevertheless, I will pray to my God for guidance.

The Reverend Mother said that under the circumstances of the sad death of my long-term friend, she has arranged to hold a memorial service the following day. This would be, she said, conducted by a friend of the Convent of the Golden Orb. She referred to him only as the Count and explained that he was a man of great understanding and experience. Following the service, she said that he wished to speak to me alone, to offer counselling and comfort. I thanked her for all the consideration and retired to my cell, where I was finally able to weep unbearable sorrow into the unyielding pillow. Eventually, I must have slept, exhausted by my tears and awoke the following morning with a severe headache and sore eyes. Nevertheless, I was duly hustled from my bed by Sister Aureole, who led me to the chapel.

~

After morning prayers, I was told to return directly to my cell, where the Count would join me shortly, and after half an hour. During which time I grew hungrier, as I had consequently been denied breakfast and no one had thought to bring any to my cell. I was also very uneasy. Why should I need to miss a meal and why should the Count (or any man within the walls of this nunnery) wish to speak to me alone in my cell? There was a knock on the door. I opened it and invited the Count to enter. Having done so, he circled his hand, indicating that I should sit upon the bed, and when I had done so, he sat by my side in the chair. I remember very little of the conversation, but he was very gentle and kindly, speaking of Susan in glowing terms and requesting me to tell him the story behind our journey to the Convent of the Golden Orb. With my head lowered to hide both my shame of running away and my sadness at the loss of my friend, I related all that had happened and begged him to allow me to return to my father's house in England. Once there, I could make my apologies and become an obedient and dutiful daughter. Finally, I hid my face in trembling hands and between deep sobs of remorse made apologies to God, Father, Susan, the Count and anyone else concerned who may be listening. I think I remember the Count patting my shoulder and speaking words of comfort. I do recall hearing his voice as though far away, telling me to look into his eyes and I have no more memories of that occasion. However, I later realised that my aching head was free from pain. From that time, the Count visited me daily, always in the same kindly manner, telling me to sit upon my bed. Then he sits in the chair beside me saying, 'Be still my child and hear me.' But what is said or takes place has been washed from my memory. Every day when the Count has left me I withdraw my diary from beneath the mattress and write all I can remember. I do this because of a deep fear that my very soul is in danger and as time passes, without these writings to prompt me, I have little lasting memories upon which to draw comfort. In this place, I am known only as Sister. My name is ISABELLA DE VILLE. There, I have written it. Not because I remember, but because my name and the address of my *father's mansion are there on the flyleaf of my diary. Please God let no one find it. Today I have vague recollections of being prepared for some sort of ceremony by Sister Aureole, in the presence of Mother Superior and Sister Marie Boudica. I was, with considerable embarrassment, divested of all my clothing and bathed in scented water that flowed from the rock wall. Having been patted dry with warm towels, I was draped in a pure white fur cloak, then taken to a room at the top of the convent the back wall of which was carved into the mountain itself. (It is that soft fur and its totally pure whiteness that has enabled me to recall with more clarity than usual. Having gripped it tightly when they stripped it from my cold body, I pulled a few hairs from the garment that now rest within* this page of my diary).

It is morning and a sparkling winter's day. The room is bare, except for a low ornately carved ebony altar, in the centre of the room, around which the Sisters stand silent and unmoving. I am led to the altar and told to lie upon it. Mother Superior stands at my head. I do as told with not a little trepidation. Time in these circumstances has little meaning, but I believe I was there for at least one hour, during which the Sisters neither moved nor spoke. Then, the ceremony apparently over, I am led still in complete silence, back to the robing room and dressed again in the apparel normally worn by noviciate sisters.

∼

The previous procedure was repeated the next day and I concentrated my mind on the white fur cloak once more. Again I am able to recall the events as they happened. I also noted that although apparently carved into the mountaintop itself, the front of the room consisted of three large windows set into a wall of stone. From my position on the altar, I was only able to see the blue skies and fast-moving feathery clouds and by concentrating on these it is possible to detach myself from the plight in which I find myself.

∼

Day three was the same as previously.

∼

Day four – it is getting more difficult to concentrate. Perhaps that is because I am not feeling well. However, I still have my diary and will continue to write daily, if only a few words.

~

Day five – I went through today's ceremony as though in a trance. Can I have come under the influence of Herr Mesmer?

~

Day six – I have had to force myself to write these words today – ceremony as previously. Must concentrate. Read my name over and over. Must remember it.

~

This is the seventh day and unimaginable horrors have begun. I am taken as previously, to what I now think of as the preparation room. But on this occasion, after the bathing, I am massaged with sweet-smelling oils. Again, the Sisters say nothing – it is as though they are dumb and deaf to my pleas for an explanation. I am once again engulfed in the white fur cloak and led to the mountaintop room, where, as before, I am obliged to lie upon the black altar.

I must remember. I must concentrate. Must write about it NOW. It is difficult.

As in the preparation room, the procedure in that menacing room with the altar also differed. Mother Superior loosened the fastenings on my white fur 'memory' cloak allowing it to fall open, leaving me naked and embarrassed. I tried to sit up, to pull the cloak around me again, but four of the Sisters, two on each side, pressed me down again, holding me in position by shoulders and legs, preventing any movement. I have some small shreds of fur in my clenched fists. Mother Superior makes soothing noises, smoothing my brow until I perforce, accept my predicament and relax. This is not so difficult, as the Sisters, until now silent, commence a soft melodic chanting that is soporific, and I find myself in a pleasant trance state. I remember the tempo changing…

'AVE MAGISTER! AVE MAGISTER! AVE MAGISTER!

Mother Superior's hand now pressed firmly on my brow, preventing me from raising my head, but standing at my feet I can just see the tall dark figure of the Count. Fear and disgust grip me as his hands slide from my toes to my thighs. Then he speaks. I cannot recall the exact words but I am sure he commenced with, 'Be still my child and hear me.'

I am so tired. I can write no more…

~

Father Gregory unbent from his reading and stood, rubbing his locked spine with both hands. Then he went to the basin of water and splashed his tired eyes, which were now red-rimmed from an hour of concentrated reading. Stretching, he again returned to the table where he bent his head on folded hands to pray.

"Holy Father in heaven I pray for your guidance in the reading of these words, for I feel they will reflect on the future life of the child. It is the duty of all of us at St Patrick's, to protect him from the evil that lies without these walls, and the seed of his father that runs within him. With the help and guidance of thou our God and your Angels, I pray that the evil will be buried deep beneath the good that we will endeavour to bring to fruition. Protect Sister Teresa oh God and give her the strength to do what is required of her in the upbringing of this child, and to keep the secret entrusted to us both, for the sake of your son Jesus Christ. Amen."

Prayers finished, Father Gregory, Prior of St Patrick's, crossed himself, knuckled his eyes and commenced to read once again.

~

…I must continue. If I stop now and allow myself to sleep, I know I shall forget. I am clutching more of the white fur in my hand that I pulled out as it was stripped from me. He penetrates me. I scream with pain until blessed blackness – then nothing. But I remember the horror and pain. They, who I thought to be my friends and protectors, held me down while that devil raped me, implanted his seed in me, and now I think – no, I know it – his child grows within me.

~

Several days have passed since I last wrote and the above words are constantly running through my mind until I fear for my sanity. Today I have once again returned to the comfort of this book of memory, the one thing to which I can refer and know the truth thereof. Since the day of 'the bad experience,' I am left alone for most of the time. Occasionally, I am allowed to walk in the grounds, always accompanied, but most of the time is spent in my room. I am no longer expected to attend services or go to the refectory for meals, which are brought usually by Sister Aureole, to my room and are of the highest quality cuisine. Today I tried to speak with Sister Aureole. I asked her to describe what Sister Joseph had seen when Susan fell from the clifftop. She was unwilling to talk and made an excuse to leave.

~

Today Sister Aureole seemed uneasy and was in less of a hurry to leave my presence than usual. So after speaking of the weather, which was developing the real warmth of summer, I once again enquired about Susan. More willing to talk to me now, Sister Aureole told me that from the grounds where Sister Joseph was tending the roses, she saw Susan walk to the clifftop and just continue walking. I was very upset and Sister Aureole pleaded with me not to tell anyone she had spoken of the matter. "Mother Superior will dismiss me or have me killed," she said and ran from the room in distress. I thought long and hard about that comment, but when I consider what has happened to me since arriving at the Convent of the Golden Orb, I must confess to believing it is possible.

~

I have not written in my diary for some six weeks and since that time Sister Aureole and I have not spoken, other than the pleasantries and thanks associated with the occasion. Although Sister Aureole always brings my meals, one of the other nuns sometimes brings my hot milk at mid-morning and last thing at night. The milk is always placed on the table and the sister who has the responsibility of delivering the beverage retreats without a word. It is now obvious that I am with child and my health is good. I do however, seem to have trouble thinking clearly, and spend a great deal of time in deep sleep.

In all this time I have not seen or heard from Mother Superior or the Count, and although relieved by this I am somewhat perturbed. I know that my future is somehow involved with that of the Count. It must in some way be connected to my pregnancy but what his plans may be, I have no idea.

~

Father Gregory skipped the next few entries. They were just short one-line entries, merely indicating that there was no change in the daily life of Lady Isabella. However, the fact that these entries were made was an indication of her continued determination to try and hold on to her sanity. Then turning to the next page he realised that the entries had increased once more and read on…

~

A week has passed, I am so bored, so depressed.

This morning, something happened to clear my head and change everything. The nun who brought my mid-morning milk kept her face hidden with her cowl, and as she entered, seemed to accidentally close the door behind her. She placed the milk then turned and caught me in her arms. It was Susan.
  "Susan – my dear friend Susan – I thought you were dead. Sister Joseph saw you fall from the cliff."
  My clever Susan hushed me, although there was no one to hear us, and proceeded to tell me her story…

That was when the doorbell roused me from what I can only describe as a trance state. I shook myself and slowly sat up, the recliner folding with more ease than my knees could manage. The bell rang again, finger firmly holding the button down. I forced myself to stand and walk to the door, leaning heavily on a walking stick for balance.
  I checked through the little glass peephole to see who was there. It was Suzanne with a box of shopping for me, so I opened the door and glanced around to check that the neighbours were not rubbernecking. Not that it would be an easy thing to do because the surrounding hedge now stands some three metres high. I will not allow Helena Rose to employ someone to cut it, for she would

have them cut it right down to less than two metres. I motion with my head for Suzanne to enter. We have not met for nearly two years, not since our divorce became absolute, and although we speak regularly on the phone, she has no idea how much I am affected by the disease.

"Oh, Mike!" She was overcome at the sight of me. It gave me great pleasure to see your tears, in my book they prove your love.

Not that you have ever denied that, although you tend to put it in a different format. You say you will always love me but dislike me intensely. Well, I guess that's reasonable enough, I'm not really a likeable chap, and if my past lives are anything to go by, I never have been particularly pleasant – except perhaps when I was Peter de Ville.

I took her hand and led her through to the kitchen.

"Put the kettle on honey and make me a pot of tea, please. A proper pot, I only ever get mugs with a tea bag these days."

You made it without any more preamble and we sat at the table sipping the delectable nut-brown beverage. For the next twenty minutes, you questioned me about the disease that was slowly debilitating and killing me, how many and what tablets I took and how things were between Helena Rose and me.

Finally, I managed to get you off that subject and tried to explain how I had, in my strange trance-state, stolen my file from Dr Jennings' office, although I am quite certain that it never really happened. The visits to the psychiatrist – yes, but the exemption certificate (surely conscription was over by that time) and stealing my stuff – no! However, I didn't feel up to explaining my search for a 'chattel wife,' for I know that part did actually happen and I was not up to being that truthful. I also tried to explain the effect my recollections were having. How easy it was now to drift off into what I can only describe as a hypnotic trance, and how the lives I experienced during those times seem more and more to be a regression into a life I have lived previously in different times. You looked at me as though I was not in my right mind. Understandable I suppose, after all, it is a pretty strange state of affairs.

However, I finally persuaded you to believe me and said I would let you have all the memory-sticks and recordings once I reached the end of the ongoing regression to Henri de Ville. We shook hands, gently, in the form of what used to be called a 'gentleman's agreement' but what I thought of as a pact between friends. You promised to peruse all the information I passed to you, thoroughly and carefully, then phone me to decide what should be done about the situation.

We said a rather awkward goodbye and you exited by the back door, leaving the garden at the side of the house and driving off, hopefully, unseen by nosy neighbours.

My snacks and a couple of bottles of spring water were carefully packed away in a plastic box with a clip-on lid and placed under a similar one that contains various papers. Water! I ask you; what sort of beverage is that for a man? However, I know full well that imbibing alcohol along with my various 'pills and potions' could serve to do more harm than good, so I am pretty careful of such things. I shall fill the bottles from the tap when they are empty. I was still determined not to eat food prepared for me by my nurse/wife – I definitely did not trust her.

Then I decided I was hungry. Suzanne's visit had given me a new lease of life, revived my spirits I guess. Perhaps it is just that I have been with someone I now know I love – can I ever repay you for the past unhappiness I have caused? I doubt it but intend to try. Anyway, what with one thing and another I decided I would cook a meal for tonight. That way, not only would I have what I wanted, but would know it was safe to eat. So I cleverly put a steak and kidney pie in the oven. Okay, maybe not so clever, I got it out of the freezer. The peas and carrots were frozen too, as I find it difficult to prepare such things. However, potatoes were not a problem for we had what Suzanne always called a 'totopoler.' It is a machine in which you place the potatoes and attach a hose to the cold-water tap, then turn it on. The inside of the container is sand-rough and the water flow sends the potatoes around and around, the centrifugal force grinding the peel from them. It is a swine to clean, however, so I left it in the sink for Helena Rose to deal with later.

That done, I made sure there was no indication of my visitor and went for a shower before Helena Rose arrived home from work.

I was very nice to her that evening, following her from the kitchen when she carried the dishes to the table, always alert to her every move as she served the food. I even managed to produce a bottle of her favourite red wine, which after watching her open it and pour a glass, I helped myself to a small amount so that we could touch glasses…etc. I am really very good at this type of deception and by the end of the meal, during which she had nearly emptied the wine bottle, Helena Rose was quite sure I thought the world of her and was physically on the mend. I encouraged her to finish off the wine, by which time she was sleepily inebriated and happy to retire.

Stupid bitch!

I was completely exhausted but had bought myself peace of mind for a short time. Strangely enough, I slept better than I had done for some time, so I guess exhaustion and a relaxed mind worked well together.

Helena Rose was very solicitous the next morning. I, however, just grunted and told her to leave my breakfast by the bedside and push off to work. She had not opened the curtains so it was dark and I cannot be sure, but I think she looked hurt and disappointed at my attitude. Did she really expect things to remain the same day after day?

I got up about half an hour later, chucked away her now soggy toast and made some more, then back to the really interesting part of my day…

I set the alarm for three hours later, settled comfortably on the recliner, closed my eyes and brought my thoughts back to the convent in Switzerland, Lady Isabella de Ville, and her faithful friend Susan.

It took longer this time and I was getting worried it wouldn't happen. That was probably the problem, I was too twitchy, expecting to fall straight into a trance. Perhaps I dozed off…then…

3

Father Gregory was still sitting at the table reading, but this time his tired eyes were put to strain even more as he read the small writing of Susan Blessed.

Susan Blessed's Diary – Switzerland

"Oh, Isabella my dear friend." I wrapped her in my arms. It was such a relief to see she was safe. I told her how from the time they separated us I had realised that all was not as it should be at the Convent of the Golden Orb. How I was set to work in the kitchens and how hard I had tried to see her. But although we were never allowed to meet, and I could not attend the ceremonies Isabella was involved in, there was talk in the kitchens. There were rumours about a man who had been involved with the convent for many years. He was known of only as the Count, and his name was whispered, for it was feared. It was said that every ten years the Count instigated an old occult ceremony. It apparently involves a young virgin of great beauty, who after certain rituals about which no one seemed to know anything, is given to mate with the Count and to bear him a child. There was much discussion about the failure of previous attempts, apparently resulting in either miscarriages or malformation of the infant. In the latter case, the child would immediately be suffocated and thrown over the cliff (the same one where I was supposedly seen to fall).

I soon realised that you, Isabella, are the chosen one this time and it was strongly believed throughout the convent that after two hundred years, this birthing would be successful. Something to do with your antecedents and such. I asked, "You are not with child are you, Isabella? Oh, please tell me no!" I remember the fear that cramped my stomach when you replied that it was a certainty, although you had little or no memory of its conception. However, when Isabella related all she could remember of the ceremonies, she confessed to feeling very strange but having no one in whom she could confide and knowing little of carrying a child within, she assumed that these feelings were commonplace. My poor darling seems unnaturally pleased to have been able to tell me these few things, and I am much worried. Then she explained about her memory lapses and showed me the diary entries that enabled her to keep some idea of what seemed to be happening to her. It is worse than I expected, for I now feel quite sure she is being drugged, probably in the milk. I believe she is right about the Count too, that man is the devil incarnate.

I try to reassure her and emphasise that we must now think about our escape. Isabella picked up the mug of milk, but fortunately, I beat her to it, tipping the liquid into the chamber pot beneath the bed. I realised then that you were unaware that your milk is always drugged to prevent you from wandering and to obviate the necessity of the Sisters keeping a constant watch over the carrier of their precious child.

Isabella asked if I was not expected to return the glass to the kitchen but I assured her that I had managed to bring the milk by pretending to be one of the Sisters, but someone else would certainly be collecting it in order to check your impassivity. I explained that I would conceal myself behind the door at that time and that you Isabella should act in a normal placid manner. Then we could plan our escape and eventual return to England.

Shortly after, Sister Aureole entered the room without knocking, and it was fortunate that we were already prepared. It was difficult for poor Isabella to achieve her normal drowsy appearance, knowing as she now did that her milk had been drugged in some manner, to keep her compliant. Today I had prevented my friend from drinking the stuff and in consequence, Isabella was somewhat more alert. Also, she is aware of me hidden behind the door. When Sister Aureole opens the door and glances around the small cell, I am glad that the day is cloudy, giving little illumination through the slit window. However, she appeared satisfied that all was as it should be and retrieving the mug left the room, closing the door behind her. I hastened to place a chair beneath the door handle to prevent anyone else from entering unexpectedly. Then we sat side by side on the bed and I told my dear friend how I had managed to re-enter the convent and promised to show her this written account of how I achieved my 'death' by falling over the cliff once we were safely away from here.

Isabella finds it difficult to grasp the evils I assured her were taking place and insists that Sister Aureole is always very kind to her, explaining that it is she who usually brings her food and has supervised her preparation for the special ceremonies. She stopped speaking as realisation struck and I nodded, saying "Yes, my dearest, she is also the one who prepares the drugged milk that shuts down your own will and ensures that you can be easily manipulated." However, she insists that I must not worry about her as Mother Superior has told her that she and the Count would take good care of her for the rest of her days.

My response I am sure surprised her. I was horrified and tried to explain that she was undoubtedly the chosen one for the Count's ten-year experiment. I reminded her that I had mentioned this before, but she had actually paid it little attention. I imagine she did not really believe it could be true. But I drew her attention to her own diary entries. Now she has learnt more and I assured her that it could mean her death – almost certainly will, if you stay here, I told her.

~

The Prior stood, stretched and poured himself a glass of red wine. He leaned back in his chair sipping the wine, swirling it around his mouth before swallowing. The next section would make reading easier as it had been printed, so draining his glass Father Gregory replaced it and bent once more to his task.

~

THE PREVIOUS PAGES WERE WRITTEN DURING THE LONG AFTERNOON. I LEFT ISABELLA'S ROOM BEFORE HER MIDDAY MEAL WAS SERVED. NOW, KNOWING MY WAY ABOUT THE CONVENT WELL AND THE DAILY WORKINGS OF ITS RESIDENTS, I WAS ABLE TO MAKE MY WAY UNOBSERVED TO A LITTLE-USED STOREROOM, WHERE I KNEW I WOULD BE UNDISTURBED. IT WAS HERE THAT I COMPLETED THE NOTES THAT I INTEND TO HAND TO MY DEAR FRIEND WHEN SHE IS ON HER WAY BACK TO ENGLAND. I HAD PREVIOUSLY HIDDEN THE QUILL AND INK THAT I HAD MANAGED TO KEEP FROM DISCOVERY ON OUR ARRIVAL. I HOPE TO HAVE THE OPPORTUNITY TO BIND THESE PAGES IN THE FRONT OF THOSE THAT I HAVE WRITTEN OVER THE MONTHS SINCE WE FIRST ARRIVED IN SWITZERLAND. WE HAVE AGREED THAT I SHALL NOT RETURN TO ISABELLA'S CELL UNTIL AFTER HER EVENING DRINK OF MILK HAS BEEN DELIVERED. THEN I WILL CONCEAL MYSELF BEHIND THE DOOR AS PREVIOUSLY UNTIL SISTER

AURIOLE HAS LEFT FOR THE NIGHT. AFTER THAT! WELL, WHO CAN TELL – I CAN ONLY PRAY AND TRUST TO MY BELOVED JOSHUA.

Oh dear, thought the prior, back to deciphering Susan Blessed's scrawl again!

The Arrival at the Convent of the Golden Orb
We stayed together for the first few days then they separated us and I was taken to what I can only describe as slave quarters. The girls who work in the kitchen and laundry were mostly young novices, only children really, for apart from me and Sister Thomasina the nun in charge, not one of them appears to have reached maturity. They are without exception from poor homes, which means that the convent will never receive any remuneration from their families. Consequently, these poor creatures are expected to work their fingers to the bone, until they reach the age of twenty when those who survive will be allowed to commence their training as noviciates to prepare them to become Sisters of the Convent of the Golden Orb. If they do attain this status, then each individual will by that time be sufficiently brainwashed to ensure their full loyalty to Mother Superior. Sister Aureole had apparently been one of these unfortunates, but far from showing the compassion of pre-knowledge to the poor girls as you might expect, she is consistently cruel and bitter. I was given to understand that Sister Aureole is the one charged with the particular security of Isabella and myself within these dark walls.

The fact that I am placed amongst those working in the kitchens, makes it a little easier for me to slip out from time to time. During this time, I am first put to preparing vegetables and it is my job to take the peelings to the bins. A local farmer feeds them to his swine and in return supplies the convent with meat and milk from his herds, sending his son to collect the bins each afternoon. I have made it my business to speak with him and to flirt outrageously. Isabella would no doubt be shocked by this revelation, but it is a very necessary step towards our escape from this place. I hear all sorts of stories in the kitchens and being unable to see or speak with Isabella, my main thoughts are how I might contact her and get us away from here.

Anyway, I continue to speak daily with the farmer's son who I have learned is named Joshua. He is as handsome as he is kind and above all is in love with me. I can feel the blood flood my body with a blush of heat as I confess in my mind that I have fallen in love with him too, and lust for his touch. In this place, such thoughts are inappropriate but confirm to me the urgency to leave it as soon as possible.

~

Joshua has today asked me to marry him and I have made arrangements to meet with him within the grounds tonight. I must make sure that I can leave with Isabella before I can accept his proposal. She is my friend and I will not abandon her in this wicked place. It is difficult to creep out but once Sister Aureole has made her rounds of our cells, she will retire to her own room, which is far away from those of the menials. I have always had an interest in the healing qualities of certain herbs and during my time here, have made good use of that knowledge to help the women around me. I put a small amount of a root that I know to be soporific in Sister Thomasina's hot milk – she will sleep well, and the girls always do so, as they are exhausted. Later, when all is quiet I will leave my cell and make my way to the kitchen. I had earlier made sure the hinges and key were well oiled, an easy thing to do in the busy kitchen, as everyone is so busy about their own tasks that they pay little attention to those of others. The only thing I have to look out for is if one of the Sisters is about. Mother Superior insists that what she chooses to call 'Guardian Sisters,' are always at their stations, in both the East and West wings. Their job is to ensure all is quiet and unmoving throughout the night. Opening the door, I made my way around the east wing, keeping close to the wall. Then I am on the hillside and there are rocky outcrops to keep me from sight. Joshua had indicated where I should meet him at the clifftop where the outcrops flattened. I had not explored in that direction before so it was with some trepidation that I climbed, and considerable joy when I saw him sitting on the ground with his feet dangling over the edge of the cliff. My love clasped me to him, pulling me down. I was flustered by this until he explained that we might be seen clearly from the convent. I told him about Isabella, how it is that we are now at the Convent of the Golden Orb, how we had been separated and the rumours of the Count that abounded. Joshua had also heard these rumours in the village and what is more, he believed them. His father has told him that over the period of his life he can recall clearly some thirteen young women who have disappeared from the village, never to be seen again, and Joshua remembers one such disappearance ten years ago. Being of an inquisitive mind he discovered that these disappearances occurred at the same time in each case – the beginning of April – the birthing planned to take place apparently, sometime in December. If these assumptions are correct, then obviously not all the birthing mothers had been culled from the villages surrounding the Convent of the Golden Orb, and my dear Isabella may already be with child. Also, the number of girls taken to the convent, were not necessarily chosen as Birth Mothers. I wondered how many of them had died in childbirth and how many murdered as being unacceptable to the Count, for sure not one of them could be allowed to leave or speak of their experience to the nuns.

We planned the escape with meticulous detail. We are all given two hours of recess once per week. My day is Friday, from ten o'clock to noon. I hate to do this to Isabella, for she will surely be told of my suicide. But it is all for the best. Joshua has lived in this area all his life, his father and grandfather before him, and he knows these mountains like the back of his hand. He also knows the caves that run through them. One such led from the lower hills and tunnels up to a ledge some ten feet below the clifftop. I now know how he had arrived at our meeting place and why he chose it. Our plan was simple. On my next recess, I am to walk up to the clifftop, making sure that one of the sisters sees where I go. I will peer over the top of the precarious drop but will actually be taking hold of a rope, the same one Joshua had fixed two nights ago, and check that he is waiting for me. Then I will step over the cliff, holding the rope for support as I abseil into Joshua's waiting arms. Whilst he hastens to remove the rope from its anchor around a lone tree, I will remove my cloak, dropping it over the ledge where it will float like a great bat until lodging on a protruding rock – evidence of my fall.

~

The plan worked perfectly and the cave within the mountain was both awe-inspiring and terrifying, in its beauty. We entered from the ledge into a cunningly hidden narrow dark tunnel, where Joshua had placed a torch. Its flickering flame gave us both light and shadows that moved like ghosts, but Joshua did not hesitate as he led me downwards, steadying my stumbling steps. We passed through a large cave the size and ambience of a cathedral with stalactites like great drapes above an altar of stalagmites that formed great pillars as they met with their downward counterparts. A narrow fissure led to a steep path, the end of which seemed to take forever, widening in places to form pools of clear water of indeterminate depth, filled from an internal flowing stream. This stream also feeds the river that flows through the village, sometimes slowly meandering over huge rocks and then gushing with white water over areas where landslides have formed waterfalls. This is an area of mountains and rocks. However, there are occasional plateaux upon which the villagers have built their homes, from which they make a living. Joshua warned me that the stream floods the runnels during March and April when the snows melt, but now in May they are in retreat making it safe to use them again. Finally, we exited through another cave at the bottom of the cliff and in fifteen minutes were safe in the farmhouse. Joshua's mother is a sweet kind lady, who immediately led me to the fire and plied me with hot food and drink before leading me to a warm bed, where I slept for a full day and night.

~

The next step is for me to return to the convent secretly, which means another trip through the mountain. The return journey will be a great deal harder and once I arrive, I shall need to keep hidden and to contact Isabella without discovery. We will then escape through the mountain, to the safety of the farmhouse once more. Joshua, together with his father this time, will be waiting for us at the cliff top, two nights hence, to give me a chance to organise things.

~

I pleaded with Isabella that we must escape and asked how often she was able to leave her room? How often was she able to be alone outside her room? Never? She thought about that and had to confess that was indeed the case. I pointed out that she was a prisoner, confined by the orders of the Count and kept secure by Mother Superior and her coven of occult nuns.

I told her that I had learnt a great deal about the Sisters of the Golden Orb and that not all of it appeared to be good, sound Christianity. They are involved in the occult to a large degree, and the convent with its nuns are merely a cover for the occult activities of the Count. I am sure that what I think of as the 'worker nuns' are definitely not included in anything outside their work and prayers and explained that they always eat separately from the main order. Their sleeping quarters are not individual cells but are shared between four. I am not quite sure why, but for some reason, I was allocated a single-occupancy cell. Perhaps it is the fact that I am older with experience of the world outside and they feared that I would tell stories of the freedom outside. A cell, as I tried to explain to Joshua and his parents, is precisely that. Each cell contains a fixed stone bench on which are a thin horsehair mattress and two blankets. The only other furniture consists of a rough chest of drawers and a crucifix on one wall. Not all the cells boast a window and the girls with these are the lucky ones, for the so-called window is merely a narrow open slit, facing North and open to the elements, so they are freezing cold. My cell had one of these slits and I soon learnt to use my habit wedged tight into the slit with the crucifix from the wall, which made things a little better. I don't know what the others do, probably the same, but it is always essential to make sure the cells are as expected before Sister Aureole makes her morning inspection at six o'clock. I was always very careful about that, especially after I heard what happened to poor Peg one morning when she overslept and Sister Sadistic found Peg's habit. The workers call her that (Sister Sadistic) behind her back of course. You probably don't know, but worker's habits are made of sackcloth, not the warmer black cloth, like yours Isabella, and Peg's had bits of straw clinging to it. She was having a jolly with Jacob the gardener and had spent most of the night with him in the barn. Poor Peg was beaten then locked in the punishment cell with only bread and water for five days. Everyone has been very careful since then, as you can imagine.

~

I peeped out of the door of my closet. It was a real relief because the cramped room was claustrophobic and although I was not too bad with that sort of thing, being shut in for so long was beginning to get to me. Nuns were still busying in the corridors and I would have to wait until vespers to be sure the coast was clear and there was less chance of being seen. I could have managed it any time, but Isabella is not up to being slippery – it's not in her nature. So I made myself as comfortable as possible and dozed off. Fortunately, I had 'acquired' some bread, cheese and fruit from the kitchen, so I was not hungry. I will continue this writing once we are safely back at the farmhouse.

~

Father Gregory knuckled his eyes, stretched his cramped limbs and eased himself from the chair, leaning hard on the tabletop.

In the distance, a bell chimed…

~

I jumped as the alarm clock clanged its waking alarm. Three hours had passed and I had read through the eyes of the old Prior what had been written in those two diaries.

Was Henri de Ville the baby, me in a previous life? If so, how am I able to learn of the incidents <u>prior</u> to my/his birth?

This is getting so scary. I wish I could just walk away from it.

Ha! That's a joke, for all I can do is hobble. At night I can go to my bed and sleep, but if during the day I relax and inevitably fall into that wonderful sleep known generally as a cat-nap, then I seem to automatically regress. It can't just be a dream, for dreams do not often follow on like a serial on the television. I have experienced the effect of waking in the middle of a dream, turning over and knowing I am half-awake, then continuing with the same dream. But those types are just of the one-off variety and like all dreams do not really make much sense. This is different. I may have said this before but my recall of the regressions is just about perfect, I can even recollect the emotions and smallest details, something that is nigh impossible with the recollection of a dream.

Yes, I know. How is it that I always set the alarm or expect the doorbell to ring unless I am aware of what will occur? Well, I have only just fully accepted what is happening. I might have had an inkling of what might be occurring and been a bit scared before, but it's only just come to me that I don't really have any control over what is happening anymore. I now believe that someone, somewhere, wants me to discover the truth – whatever that might be.

With that in mind, I shall continue. Anyway, I am on a timed fuse that might go off at short notice blasting me into oblivion, but I suspect it will last for as long as is needed to complete what I am beginning to think of as my quest. The quicker I can get through the regressions, the sooner I shall be free of this aching body that holds my very essence prisoner.

I am anxious to know what happens during the life of Henri, but apparently, I first need to know what brought Isabella back to the Priory of St Patrick's.

I lowered my heavy, awkward body onto the stool that is fixed into the shower and let the hot jets hit it like so many needles until the water begins to chill. Then I turned it off and draped myself in a towelling dressing gown. It obviates the necessity of the effort required to dry oneself.

Individually frozen Lasagne will do for dinner tonight, with broccoli and carrots. I will swap plates with Helena Rose at the last moment. That way, I shall be sure I am not poisoned. That way she might be! Can't risk that, I'm afraid I need her, so I will do the swap in front of her, then if it has been poisoned she won't eat it and I shall know.

Dinner was very tasty. We both ate our Lasagne and commented on how good it was. That put me in a good mood, so the evening was spent pleasantly listening to Haydn's Toy Symphony and Beethoven's sixth, whilst playing chess. I won of course, but I must confess it was close.

Slept well and after the usual kerfuffle of getting dressed, had my breakfast, then, being anxious to find out more about Isabella and Susan, I once again set the alarm for three hours and relaxed on the recliner, eyes closed, breathing evenly…one…two…

4

The old Prior was once again sitting at his table with the two diaries spread open before him. He drew the writings of Isabella towards him, they would be easier on the eyes. Outside, the sun twinkled with midday brightness.

~

Since my dear Susan has left me for a few hours, I am going to write more in my memory book as I am thinking much more clearly today. I feel so much better since I stopped drinking the milk. I still cannot really believe that Sister Aureole would drug me. On the other hand, if the Count controls Mother Superior then presumably all the other nuns involved are also under his guidance through her and would consequently be unable to disobey his command. Tonight, Susan and I will leave the convent through the caves. I am fearful of that journey. Fearful of being caught. What would happen to me then? What would the Count do? I can answer that myself. I would be confined in a closed room at the centre of this place of dread, with a guard night and day to ensure I consumed all that was given to me, and no one other than my captors would be able to converse with me. The Count would visit me regularly once again. I would be speedily hypnotised by him for I now realise that the words he spoke to me, 'Be still my child and hear me,' were those that lulled me immediately under his control. No doubt also his wandering hands would explore my inert body, wherever they preferred.

I have made a package of the few belongings I wish to take with me. My bible and quills (I will not risk carrying ink as the journey may well lead to its spillage) and a set of undergarments. Susan says she will be able to provide normal clothing for me, so I will leave my wimple and take only what is necessary for warmth and propriety.

Now I must place this book in the bundle and will sit quietly, in prayer, until Susan comes once more.

~

Father Gregory stood, stretching his long limbs and poured wine from the carafe. He sipped the drink and returned to the diaries. Back to the papers written by Susan Blessed, a magnifying glass was in his hand this time, making the reading an easier task…

~

I must have slept for longer than I intended, for it was quiet when I awoke only one candle at each end of the corridor gave any light, from which I deduced the time to be after 9 o'clock.

Isabella would believe I had deserted her. That indeed proved to be the case for when I entered the room, she was pacing to and fro and was in a very nervous state. Sister Aureole had already collected Isabella's empty cup and the only comment she had made was to wish her God's Peace for a blessed night. But there was no time for recriminations and I made haste to guide my friend from her room. I carried only Isabella's small reticule that she had managed to secrete, which contained her diary and writing materials, and to which I had added my own notes. I insisted that we remove and carry our shoes to ensure silence as we made our way through the darkened corridors toward the kitchens. Here I paused, for the Convent's cook, Sister Thomasina, had her sleeping quarters at one end of the kitchen and although I knew she was a heavy sleeper, there was no point in taking risks. The hinges had been well oiled, for I had done this myself, but I discovered that the two bolts that had not previously in my experience been drawn were now firmly closed. Fortunately, they were also free-moving, but although the bottom one could be easily manipulated, the one at the top required that I stood on tiptoe. I, therefore, had less control and the bolt was heavy and awkward to move whilst trying to balance at the same time. However, it was managed successfully. Only the key to turn in the lock now and we would be outside. I hesitate to say we would be free. Before those words could be safely uttered, we had first to negotiate our way through the grounds, hoping no watchers would see us, and then travel through the caves to the safety of Joshua's family farm.

Drawing Isabella quickly through the door I placed my finger on my lips to indicate silence, and we gratefully replaced our shoes, buttoning only enough to ensure they would not trip us. We stood for a while to ensure our exit had not been heard, then taking my friend's hand I led the way I had taken when first meeting with Joshua at the clifftop.

My Joshua was waiting for us and hastened to lower first Isabella over the cliff edge into the waiting arms of his father. Then, after holding me close and kissing me deeply he lowered me, removed the rope from the tree and clambered down himself. The journey through the caves took longer this time as Isabella was nervous and somewhat impeded by her pregnancy, so needed much encouragement and assistance as we travelled through the damp dark caves. Nevertheless, we did eventually arrive safely at the farmhouse and the warm welcome of Joshua's dear Mama. Indeed a kinder, more loving creature I have never met and I already think of my future mother-in-law as Mama, which she instructed me to call her as soon as we told her of our intention to wed.

When Isabella realised that I would not be travelling back to England with her she was rather sad, however, she was glad for me and already loved Joshua and his family. We were to be married when Joshua's Uncle Hans, who is a prosperous banker in Geneva, paid his annual visit to his sister for two weeks at the beginning of July, with his wife and two daughters. Their company did much to improve Isabella's spirits and she was now showing clear signs of her pregnancy. The girls, Maria and Eugenie were respectively 17 and 15 years of age and appeared to have a far greater knowledge of the world than did either of us. I supposed it was because they lived in a busy city and the fact that their parents entertained constantly. They soon took Isabella in hand, providing her with articles of clothing from their own closets, insisting she keep them and styling her hair in the modern fashion. She was by the end of their vacation, looking much more like her old self. No, that is not right. She was looking different. Naturally, she had put on weight but it agreed with her. The good food, happy home and companionship all served to put a light in her eyes and spring in her step.

Thus it was that when Uncle Hans and his family left the farmhouse, Isabella went with them, as governess to the girls. It was intended that Maria and Eugenie, together with their mother and governess, would be travelling to visit their Aunt Lucille in Devonshire England. And that is the end of my involvement with my dear friend Isabella de Ville, for my life henceforth is here on the farm with my true love.~

One minute I was reading the diary of Susan Blessed through the eyes of Prior Gregory at St Patrick's and the next was back in the familiar surroundings of my home. Glancing at the nineteenth-century long-case clock I perceived that it was 11 o'clock. On this occasion only one hour had elapsed. I tried relaxing again, after all, I was accustomed to a period of three hours passing each time I regressed into my trance state, but apparently, this was all I was getting this time.

Feeling I had been done out of allotted information and not a little irritated by this state of affairs I roused myself and shuffled into the kitchen.

Damn! Pain shot through my hand as I gripped the tap. I adjusted the pressure to the palm and fingers three and four, turning anticlockwise and releasing the gush of cold water into the kettle-jug. Just one litre, enough for a mug of tea, even holding the kettle under the tap was an effort nowadays and I have to resort to balancing it on the edge of the washing-up bowl. I had just made my drink and rinsed the spoon, time for a painkiller I think, which was when the phone rang. I jumped, spilling hot liquid over my hand, swore and placing the now dripping mug on a magazine, lifted the handset.

"Deville Speaks!" I exclaimed in a voice loud enough to make the caller's ears ring. A wasted effort however as it was only Helena Rose and she is well aware of my answering technique.

"Are you alright darling?" she said. "You were still asleep when I left this morning so I'm just checking. Is there anything I can bring you tonight?"

I told her to get me a Model Engineering magazine. Then the real reason for her call came forth.

"Oh, by the way, I've been asked to attend the Company exhibition this weekend. They want me to be in charge of the stand and we're invited to the dinner dance on Saturday evening. I've said yes…" She trailed off, knowing well what my reaction would be, but hoping for a break. I kept her waiting for a few seconds longer…just to increase the stress she was experiencing, then told her magnanimously, that she was well aware that such an activity was beyond my inclination, and indeed capabilities, but that she was welcome to avail herself of the invitation. This threw her somewhat. A whole forty-eight hours all to myself, what a relief, I shall be able to make real headway and perhaps even complete this strange regression thing.

"But, darling, can you manage on your own for two days?"

"Of course I can. You take advantage of the chance of a break Helena Rose, for once I am wheelchair-bound that will mean you may have to give up work altogether to look after me."

I spoke as pedantically as I could, rubbing in the fact that she would in the near future have to spend all her time looking after me. Helena Rose would hate that.

That night was peaceful, my nurse/wife being excited about her forthcoming break, although it was supposed to be a working weekend. I wondered if she had a boyfriend on the side, after all, I had been just that (her bit on the side, as she had been mine) before Suzanne left and I moved Helena Rose in to look after me.

I determined that I would spend the next day, Thursday, getting my notes together. It was becoming more difficult to type and I needed to rest my aching hands regularly. I typed in my password, it wouldn't do for my wife to read this – she'd probably get a couple of doctors to sign the appropriate papers and have me incarcerated. It would certainly suit her down to the ground. She'd have control of my assets (quite considerable) and me out of the way. Do they still do that I wonder? Probably not – PC and all that gumph. Helena Rose is not aware that I have made a will in which I have left a large chunk to medical research. I have of course made sure she will be comfortable, it's the least I can do since she has to put up with me on a daily basis. I've tried to look after Suzanne too, she will be annoyed and might refuse to accept it, but that's up to her and Helena Rose's displeasure makes it worthwhile to me.

That night Helena Rose was home early, having been allowed the afternoon off to prepare for an early start on Saturday morning. She had apparently spent a couple of hours at the hairdressers and I must confess the result was pretty good. She hasn't nice long thick hair like Suzanne of course, but her short urchin cut suited the rather hard face and pale blue eyes. I could see she'd had the roots bleached too; the pale blond looked good on her.

After making us a steak and kidney pie with mashed potatoes, carrots and greens, Helena Rose immediately threw herself into sorting out clothes for the weekend, then soaking in a pleasantly perfumed bubble bath for an hour. I wasn't worried about being poisoned by her this time, as she was far too excited to bother with any thoughts about me. It was only nine o'clock when she came into my room to say goodnight.

"I've got to be on the move at six," she told me. "My boss is picking me up in his Jaguar at seven and I want to make sure you are comfortable before I go."

"Just go," I told her. "If I'm asleep, don't you dare wake me up, getting a decent sleep is difficult enough without being woken unnecessarily, I am quite capable of making myself comfortable."

"Well, make sure you've got your mobile close to hand all the time, and don't hesitate to call me or Dr Richard if you have any problem."

I assured her I would be very careful and eventually she kissed my cheek and retreated upstairs to bed. I heard the television when it was turned on, but she kept the sound down low and I eventually settled myself down and fell asleep.

In the morning, I heard Helena Rose moving around and feigned sleep as she leaned over me. I thought she might try to shake me awake, but after a few seconds, she sighed (was it with relief or frustration) and left the room. A short while later, I heard a car draw up, my door was opened as she peeped in again then it closed quietly. The front door opened then closed, and I heard 'the boss's Jaguar' drive off. I was finally to be left in peace for two whole days and one night. I gave a heartfelt sigh of relief and dragged myself out of bed; I didn't want to waste one moment's precious time.

~

By ten o'clock I had done all the necessaries, bathroom, dressing, breakfast and sorting out the necessary items for my next session of regression. I set up my voice-activated recorder – just in case – and fixed the alarm clock to ring at 12.30 pm. Then, getting comfortable in the old recliner I relaxed and allowed myself to drift into the world of Father Gregory, Prior of St Patrick's...

5

Father Gregory was in the chapel of St Patrick's, sitting on the hard plank of a pew that over the ages had indentations where monks had been seated regularly at least three times a day. He prayed silently, gazing at the exquisitely carved crucifix from which the eyes of Christ seemed to stare back at him, appearing to speak in the Prior's mind, guiding him.

A gentle rustle beside him drew his attention.

"Ah Sister Teresa, God Bless you."

"And yourself, Father," she replied, remaining in supplication, awaiting the Prior's pleasure before speaking again.

"I have read most of the diaries, Sister, all of that written by Susan Blessed. I now have to complete that of Lady Isabella then we two shall decide what is to be done with the babe. At this time on the morrow, would you be so kind as to meet with me in my room, so we can have before us those diaries, together with my own notes and any you may have seen fit to make."

"Thank you, Father. I will be pleased to meet with you but have put nothing in writing as I feel that what *can* be read *might* be read and it will favour neither the child nor ourselves if what we know were to be made available to all."

"Your wisdom and womanly common sense do you credit Sister Teresa, for which I thank you. Until the morrow then."

He placed his hand on the head of Sister Teresa saying, "May God protect and guide you in His light, Sister."

Then, slipping from the pew and genuflecting before the Cross, Father Gregory made his way from the chapel and returned to the tower room. Taking a small brass key from his pocket the Prior unlocked a door almost hidden in the panelled wall and removed a package that proved to be the diaries of Lady Isabella and Susan Blessed.

He laid them in an orderly manner on the table, poured some ruby wine into a chalice and seated himself. Taking a draught of the wine, he leaned over the books and prepared to continue reading.

Lady Isabella's Diary – continued

I am writing this whilst sitting at the table in the comfortable farmhouse of Farmer Gelberger. His wife has begged me to call her Hannah and she is the kindest of women. I have been given a bed in Susan's room with sheets and enough blankets to keep me really warm. But not only that, Hannah placed in my bed a warming-pan, a luxury I have not experienced since leaving my father's house, for although it is July here, in the mountains, the nights are chilly. The farmhouse is large but quaint, with balconies and overhanging eaves that are painted in bright yellows and reds. Hannah's brother is to visit soon with his family, two daughters I believe, but I am assured there will be sufficient room and I am not inconveniencing them in any way. Susan is already accepted as their daughter and the marriage to Joshua is to take place when his uncle arrives.

But I must record my journey from the Convent of the Sisters of the Golden Orb. Sister Aureole did not even bother to knock when she came to collect my empty mug. I had placed it on the table, having first emptied it and was curled beneath the blanket facing away from the door, feigning sleep. I heard her step and prayed I would not do anything silly to alert her of my wakefulness. However, although I sensed her leaning over me, she was obviously satisfied and retreated, closing the door silently. I remained still for what seemed an hour but was probably only minutes, then dressed with the exception of my shoes, which Susan had instructed me to carry in order not to make any unnecessary noise that might disturb the nuns. I was pacing back and forth when Susan eventually arrived. We were on our way to freedom at last.

All went well until Susan placed a finger to her lips and I remembered she had told me that the convent cook slept close by. I nodded my understanding and all remained quiet; we made our way through the door, stopping to replace our footwear before continuing up towards the cliff. Joshua was waiting for us and Susan introduced us – he is such a nice young man and obviously adores her. Then came the awful drop – I have no head for heights, but Mr Gelberger was right there on the ledge to catch me and he hustled me to the safety of the cave where I waited for Susan. He bid me remain whilst he assisted Susan and Joshua. And that long walk through the caves! I am afraid I must have been a trial to my dear friends.

There! When I read over what I wrote about my friends, I realised that in that short time, I already recognised Joshua and his Papa as my friends. Is that not amazing? Joshua led us unerringly through dark tunnels that ran through the mountain from cave to cave with Susan close behind him and Mr Gelberger supported me all the way, often preventing me from slipping. However, despite the dangers and my trepidation I clearly recall the ethereal beauty of the stalactites and stalagmites, some hanging like great drapes, others reminding me of icicles hanging from the eaves of the convent in winter. There were also streams, some of which were mere trickles over which we jumped with relative ease, but others were roaring waterfalls and raging rivers with water beaten rocks smoothed over the ages. We had to clamber behind one waterfall. It was cold, wet and slippery. I could not have accomplished this alone for I must surely have fallen had not Susan held my hand and walked before me while Papa Gelberger steadied me from behind. Facing toward the cliff we shuffled crab-wise along the narrow ridge, water tumbling behind us to the rocks below. When we reached the other side I was trembling but Joshua insisted we did not tarry, as being wet and cold we needed to keep moving in order to maintain the circulation of our blood. He is not only handsome but also wise beyond his years. Scrambling downward over rocks and around lakes purported to be deeper than the mountains are high. It was an experience I would prefer not to go through again. But given that and the Convent of the Golden Orb, I believe I would once again choose the former. Eventually, we entered a cave of gigantic proportion and of awe-inspiring beauty, but Joshua hurried us across to where a gleam of light crept through the gloom. At first, it was a narrow strip but as we drew nearer it widened until we could see the cave entrance, or in our case I suppose, its exit. In fact, it was well hidden from the outside, being very narrow and covered by hanging vines. We saw the light because just inside the cave Joshua's father had thought to place a lantern. The old gentleman clapped his hand on the shoulder of his son saying, "well done," hugged Susan and placed a kiss in the air on each of my cheeks. Then together we walked across a field, through a small wood of pines and along a pathway to the farmhouse.

Joshua's Mama fussed over all of us and hastened to place a delicious meal before us. I have not eaten so much, with such pleasure for many a day and fear my manners failed when I fell asleep at the table. Dear Hannah was not offended however and Susan helped me to bed, where I slept for twelve hours or more. Susan was sitting on her bed, sewing a trousseau for her wedding and her smile made me feel more alive than I had in ages, but that might have been partly due to the fact that my body was now clear of drugs. No, I am sure it was just having my friend by my side once more, albeit for a short while. She fetched me hot water and helped wash my hair and body. Such a relief to feel clean and fresh once again. I looked for my clothes, the habit being all I had, but Susan had bundled it up and provided me with undergarments and a simple dress of her own. Then down we went again to yet another of Hannah's superb meals. After the silence to which I had become accustomed, I found it difficult to join in with the constant merry chatter that accompanied the meal. This family discussed everything, from farm matters to the forthcoming visit of Uncle Hans. They sound charming and I look forward to meeting with them. Meanwhile, I decided to do all I could to help Hannah. In the next week, I learnt to cook and keep house. I also watched Susan as she milked the cows alongside her fiancée, she would be a fine farmer's wife and although sad for myself I was extremely happy for my friend.

We had all been busy preparing for the visitors and at last, they arrived. Uncle Hans is younger than his sister, but the family resemblance is obvious. He is a round jolly man with a ruddy complexion, a great deal of red hair and a bushy beard of the same colour. His wife Elspeth is completely the opposite, being a thin delicate-looking lady with pale blue eyes and almost translucent skin. This appearance however is misleading. She is a strong matriarch who obviously leads the family with a rod of iron encased in a velvet glove. Nevertheless, Elspeth is a delightful person, as are her two daughters Maria and Eugenie. I have become great friends with the girls and because of this, the plan for my return to my father's house has been arranged. I am to travel with Elspeth, as governess to the girls, to England.

But first, there is to be a wedding and I am to be maid of honour. The two girls have made me accept some of their clothes and this includes one beautiful dress belonging to Maria. She is the older of the two and is inclined to resemble her father, having his robust build and red hair that seems to have a will of its own. Hence Maria's clothes are nearer my size than those of her diminutive sister. Their mother, Elspeth has kindly made alterations to the garment where necessary and I feel like a princess when wearing the green brocade. That colour has always been a favourite of mine. Susan is to wear Hannah's wedding dress that she has carefully preserved over some twenty-five years of marriage. As she commented, "It will certainly never fit this body again." Some alterations were necessary however as Hannah was never as small as Susan.

Everything was perfect. The local priest married Susan and Joshua in his small church, and at the end of the service, they were greeted by all their neighbours and showered with petals. Susan was as pretty as a picture and Joshua was a proud handsome bridegroom. Trestle tables had been set up in a field at the back of the farm and everyone was invited to a feast fit for a king. Such a happy day and one I shall remember for the rest of my life.

There is much to be done before we set forth at the end of next week. Hans will accompany us to Geneva and see us safely on our way to France, where we are to board the ship that will carry us to England. At first, we are to stay in Devonshire with Elspeth's sister Lucille, and from thence we will make plans for my return to Worcestershire. I will therefore put this journal aside until we once again reach the land of my birth.

I fear meeting my father again, but Hannah assures me that love for his only child will surely overcome any past anger. I do hope she is right.

~

There followed a long gap here, then Isabella's diary continued…

Isabella De Ville – England

I am writing this in my old room at my father's house. The door is locked and I feel as much of a prisoner here as I did at the Convent of the Golden Orb in Switzerland. The difference is only that I am not watched or drugged. The woman who has been employed as my personal maid delivers my food. Her name is Pauline and although she rarely speaks is efficient in her duties. However, there is no possibility of any form of friendship between us. Pauline is at least twice my age, her thin face permanently set in an expression of such meanness that I fear to question her regarding my own situation. Her person is so thin that she might appear able to slide through the gap beneath my door, and if she were standing sideways one might miss seeing Pauline altogether. I imagine my father chose her with this in mind. But I will not write of my present situation, rather *that of my journey from Switzerland to England in the company of my dear friends Maria and Eugenie and their dear Mama, Elspeth.*

Saying our adieus to Susan, her new husband Joshua and his kindly parents was perhaps the most difficult thing I have ever done. I have been so happy and felt so secure at the farm but realise that undoubtedly the Count will have ordered that I be found. This can only place the Gelberger family in danger and I do not wish to have any such thing on my conscience. Uncle Hans accompanied us to Le Havre in France and saw us safely aboard the ship that was to carry us to Southampton England. I will not write about that sea trip, as I fear I was extremely unwell for the most part, suffering the mal de mere. Once again I know not what I would have done without my dear friends, who with no thought to themselves, tended, mopped up and comforted me continually.

On arrival at Southampton, being once more on terra firma, I recovered quite quickly and we boarded a train that would take us to the West Country and after many hours, by coach to the Devonshire village where we were to stay with Elspeth's sister Lucille. In appearance the sisters are completely different, Lucille being a plump, rosy, bouncy sort of person. However, in character, they are very similar – being strong-willed and quietly domineering. Lucille is a widow, her husband having died only six months previously, this being the reason for the visit of Elspeth and the girls. She is not given to moaning and mourning, however, saying that she did with all that saying goodbye in the first month, but now there was a farm to run, and cows would not milk themselves. She had two men who helped with the heavy work, they being willing to work for the woman who had been the wife to a good master. It is not considered reasonable for a man to be in the employment of a woman in these times, so says much for the character of Aunt Lucille. (I was asked to treat her as my own Aunt, like Maria and Eugenie. A thing I was delighted to do).

I was now seven months pregnant and it was decided that Elspeth would accompany me to my father's home. I said a tearful goodbye to Aunt Lucille, whom I had come to love dearly, for she was a motherly soul, although not having been blessed with children of her own. Maria and Eugenie promised to write to me and we were determined to meet again sometime in the future. (But who knows what the future holds?)

In the coach from the station to my father's mansion, Elspeth tried to explain to me what I might expect regarding the birth of my child. I knew little of these facts, only what I had learnt from Susan, and her knowledge was not that much greater than my own. I was frightened and begged her to allow me to stay within her family. I was sure Aunt Lucille would give me a home and I would work with her on the farm. But it was not to be, I feel that there is a deeper reason for the urgent necessity to house me within my father's home before the birth became imminent, but Elspeth would not or could not disclose it.

The coachman was asked to wait and we mounted the steps to the great door, pulling the bell to announce our arrival. Old Norman gasped to see me. The butler had been with the De Ville family for as long as I can remember, certainly before I was born, and he was totally loyal to my father. Elspeth stood tall and said, "Well, my man, do you intend to keep us standing here all day?" With that, we were admitted and bidden to wait in the foyer while Norman informed my father of our presence.

My father ignored me completely, looking at Elspeth and saying, "So you've delivered the baggage. Well! What are you staring at? See the lady back to her coach Norman then take that creature to her room and make sure you lock the door securely."

Elspeth tried to speak but my father had turned his back to her and strutted away. She tried to embrace me but taking her elbow in a firm grip, Norman led her through the door to her coach. I stood rooted to the spot and raised my hand as she turned and waved to me. That was the last I saw of the kind family I had adopted as my own for such a short few months.

So here I am. Pauline was employed the very next day – it is almost as though my father was expecting me – could he have known the Count? I do feel that it is quite possible.

I awoke from sleep this afternoon with a dreadful cramping pain in my stomach. When it retreated I gathered my diary to me and made this entry. I knew from what Elspeth had told me that I had started the birthing process and when later I felt more cramps I looked at my clock to see the timing of them. It was about one hour. Another cramp occurred but the time between was less and when only half an hour later I felt a further agonising pain I covered my book and rang for Pauline.

I have another break between the pains that are now occurring much more frequently, Pauline has gone to carry the news of the impending birth to my father. I am wondering why?

Another break between the pains occurred, but I now know why it was necessary for my father to be informed. I am to be delivered to the Hospice at *the Priory of St Patrick's, which is where all this started when Susan and I escaped from my father's desire to marry me to an old man whom I disliked intensely.*

Earlier I wondered that my father seemed to expect my return – now I am sure of it – why else would I be taken back to the Priory?

That was the final entry in Isabella's diary.

~

At this point, there was a knock at the door.

Father Gregory called, "Come in," and Brother John entered.

"Father Prior, there is a gentleman at the door demanding to speak with you."

"Demanding? Do you have his name, Brother John, and what is it he wishes to speak about?"

"He refuses to tell me anything and will only converse with you Prior. Forgive me Father but the man has about him an aura and it bodes no good."

"His appearance, Brother, describe him to me, please."

"He is tall, with prominent cheekbones and penetrating eyes into which I struggled not to look, for I felt their pull when first I looked at him when opening the door. I feared he would grasp my mind and control my actions."

Brother John looked sheepish as he recalled these feelings, then pulling himself together again continued.

"He has black hair worn flat to his head with a widow's peak low on his forehead, level with a narrow sharp nose and a wide thin-lipped mouth. He is dressed entirely in black, relieved only by a priest's collar, which is crimson like blood rather than the usual white. I can think of nothing else, Father, except that I will pray for your safety in his presence."

This perturbed the good Prior, for he felt in his bones that his visitor was none other than the Count of whom he had been reading and of whom he had lately heard rumours, definitely to the disadvantage of that gentleman. He thought for a while, then…

"Thank you, Brother John, your prayers may well be needed. Please show the gentleman to the chapel, I will join him there shortly."

The Prior bent his head in prayer, locked away all the papers on his table and descended the stairs that led directly to the vestry behind the altar. The man was standing by the door, his sardonic face revealing momentarily, the way in which he viewed this sacred place. Prior Gregory moved forward.

"Won't you join me, sir," he said, standing in the aisle between the front pews. The visitor hesitated, then strode towards him. The Prior crossed first himself then the air between the two of them, keeping his eyes averted from those of the person he now found himself thinking of as The Count…

…then having received no response.

"I am Father Gregory, Prior of St Patrick's, may I enquire as to your name and business?"

"My name is of no importance Prior; my business concerns a young woman who was brought by her father to this place for the purpose of giving birth to my son. That child *must* be handed to me."

Prior Gregory interrupted him, "A new-born child would need to be nurtured by his mother for a period of at least six months, or so I am told."

"His! His, then I do have a son! Praise be to the Master. Come then Prior, take me to him immediately, I will arrange for his nurturing henceforth."

"Ah, sir! I regret that the birth was not an easy one and ended in death. I regret to inform you of this, sir…"

The rage of his visitor was palpable. He bellowed such profanities that the Prior was obliged to cover his ears. Indeed, he cowered, backing away from the man until he felt the altar behind him, which he hastened to put between them. Brother John was right, the man had an aura about him that was clearly visible – it was the grey aura of evil, tinged around the edges with flames of anger. Sparks flew from his fingertips as he raged, the crucifix behind the Prior crashed to the stone floor but was unharmed and Father Gregory picked it up, holding it forth towards the man standing before him, whom he now felt sure, to be none other than the Count. He felt weak and was trembling, but the good Prior held the heavy crucifix up before him and his voice was firm with the strength of a younger man and the protection of his Guardian Angel, through the God whom he had worshipped diligently for most of his life.

"In the name of the Father, Son and Holy Ghost I command you to leave this place and go forth from whence you came!"

With a final batch of sparks from his hand that fell short of the Prior, the Man in Black said, "I curse you and the Priory of St Patrick's for five centuries," then turned and was gone.

The Prior was trembling when he reached his room once more. He poured himself a mug of red wine, which he drank with more speed than was usual. When he felt calm once more he called for Brother John, whom he knew would be waiting.

"That man is never again to be admitted to these sacred acres, Brother John, and ensure that all our brethren are aware of that. Would you also find Sister Teresa and ask her to go to the chapel at her earliest convenience. And Brother, please ensure that the message is given to her directly by yourself, letting no one else hear what you say. In fact, if possible, pass the message without being seen by anyone but Sister Teresa."

Brother John nodded and withdrew. The Prior knew that he would do as asked and keep his own counsel for, although young, Brother John was intelligent, devoted and entirely dependable. He was also the Prior's nephew, son of his deceased sister. John had been placed under the guardianship of his uncle after the death of his parents when he was still a baby. They had been inflicted by a virulent fever, which by some miracle bypassed the fifteen-month-old child.

The good Prior made his way back to the chapel to await Sister Teresa. They had much to discuss. He knelt before the altar in prayer, which was where Sister Teresa found him an hour later.

"I am so sorry, Father," she said, "I had duties to perform in the hospice, so although Brother John gave me your message I was unable to leave the convent until now."

"The fault is mine, Sister, for disturbing your normal working in the hospice, but I received an unexpected visitor." He hesitated. "Although he would give no name, I knew the man. It was the man referred to in the diaries as the Count, and he claimed to be the father of our infant."

Sister Teresa gasped. "He will try to take the child and educate him in the ways of the devil." She crossed herself, muttering a prayer.

"I think not, Sister. I gave him the impression that both child and mother died during the birth. I have asked God's forgiveness and did not actually tell a lie. I merely told him I regretted the birth was not an easy one and had ended in death. He certainly believed that both had died as indicated by his rage, so provided we take the greatest care to conceal him from the attention of the outside world, the young man should be safe enough here."

"What would you have me do, Father?"

"Will it be possible for you to take sole care of the child, Sister, until he is, say, five years of age, at which time he can enter the Priory to commence his education?"

"It will be difficult, Father, but only two other Sisters are aware of his survival at the present time, just the three of us who work in the hospice. There used to be four of us until Sister Anna Maria died. Mother Superior considered it unnecessary to replace her. Another four Nuns work in the kitchens, two more do the cleaning, except for individual cells of course, which we attend to ourselves. Then Sister Serena and Sister Margarita are very close to Mother Superior and work directly with her in the administration of the convent and hospice."

She paused. "Father?"

"What concerns you, Sister? You must be absolutely open with me, for we two have a great responsibility ahead of us."

"I am worried about Sister Margarita – her connection with the Sisters of the Golden Orb – and it was Sister Serena who took the girls to Switzerland in the first place, so inevitably Mother Superior must also be aware of the situation. It means that all knowledge of the child must be withheld from them for his safety."

"Do you think they may be involved with the Golden Orb people?"

"If not directly involved Father, they may be in communication with them, and that means that dreadful man as well. It will be almost impossible to keep the presence of a child from those three, they go where and when they choose and it is not natural for a child to keep silent, or still for any length of time."

"Let us pray, Sister Teresa, for guidance, for only God in his wisdom can find a solution to this problem now."

They knelt – prayed and thought of what must be done. After some time, they sat again on the hard wooden pew, turning to face each other. Father Gregory spoke first.

"Sister Teresa, in this instance it is proper for you to raise your head, for we are both equal in the task before us."

"Father Prior, I am not worthy to look into your eyes."

"At this time and when we discuss the boy, we should consider our situation to be equal and therefore any decisions must be made without deception. That can only be achieved if we are able to see the truth in the eyes of each other, for surely the eyes contain our souls."

She nervously raised her head, then with more confidence made the sign of the cross, saying, "God willing," then continued speaking.

"Lady Isabella de Ville became very agitated after telling me her secret and ensuring that I had the diaries safe. She begged me to keep their contents to myself alone and said that should a man dressed all in black, with a crimson cravat, the Count, ever appear at the Priory." Sister Teresa paused. "Appear – that was her very word, Father, not visit as you or I would say, and I instinctively knew exactly what she meant." She paused again.

"She said that we must never, never look into his eyes. I imagine she was warning me that he could take my very will and use me to his own ends."

"Fortunately, you had read the diaries and were aware of that danger, so thank God you are still aware and able. But the danger is there, perhaps from those within these walls Father Prior."

The good Prior nodded his understanding.

"Only we two will ever know who the father of Henri de Ville is, and that name is never to be spoken within the walls of the Priory of St Patrick's. You and I will meet to discuss the progress of the child every day, and we will pray that God places our good intentions and influence of this Godly Priory, in the heart of Henri de Ville, removing all tainted influence from his heart."

~

It happened that on the following day, a young woman was brought to the confines of the hospice where she gave birth to a stillborn son, her life's blood flowing from her anguished body, thus joining him in death.

Sister Teresa met with the Prior the following day.

"Father Gregory, I have to inform you of a stillborn birth at the hospice yesterday, during which the mother also died. With your agreement, I feel it would be beneficial to pass little Henri as being her child, which should avoid any further difficulties."

"That is splendid, Sister! God forgive me! May they both rest in peace. There is only one day between their births and I take it that Mother Superior and those closest to her are aware of the death of the young woman but not that of her child."

"I have endeavoured to tell no untruths except by omission and for the sake of the soul of little Henri will allow that to continue. I attended to the young woman entirely by myself so no one else will need to be involved in the deception. But it is now essential that we never use the full name of Henri de Ville."

"Your wisdom once again amazes me, Sister. What was the young woman's name and what do we know of her background?"

"She was the youngest of five daughters of a Farmer Grayer, being only fifteen years old. I understand she ran away with a Romani labourer that her father employed last summer. What area she came from I do not know, and her Romani husband is long gone with his family. I, therefore, took it upon myself to prepare her for burial and have tucked the babe in with her. No one will know it is there. Henri should be known as simply Brother Henri for the rest of his life – God willing."

So the deception was agreed upon and little Brother Henri began his life at the Priory of St Patrick's.

~

The alarm rang, jerking me from my trance. I had been in a comatose state on the recliner for the last three hours, not moving, and found it extremely difficult to encourage my stiff body into movement. Closing the footrest proved difficult and I had to lever myself into an upright position before I was able to slam it back.

A flash of lightning caused me to squint and the great roll of thunder that followed almost immediately made me jump, twisting my neck and adding yet another pain. I must stop dwelling on this diseased body, but I am only fifty-six and feel thirty-odd years older.

Enough of that!

Remembering that the next couple of days were free of Helena Rose's presence, I found some rolls in the freezer and thawed out three of them in the microwave. There were just a couple of slices of ham left in the fridge (use by date – today) so I used them, putting some cheese in the third roll, together with lettuce and tomato. A pot of tea completed a tasty lunch sitting at the kitchen table with my newspaper spread over most of it, a procedure that SHE strongly objects to. I read about politics, murders and mayhem throughout the world, which made me feel no better, so I rinsed my crockery and cutlery and returned to what had effectively become my bedsitting room.

I re-entered the room, reaching for my voice-operated recorder, where it rested on the coffee table at the side of my recliner. I did a double-take, for alongside it lay two books. One was bound in fine burgundy leather with spirals on the covers in tooled gold. The other was a mishmash of odd pieces of paper stitched and tied with wool between two mismatched pieces of board. I recognised them immediately as the diaries of Lady Isabella de Ville and Susan Blessed. I had seen them before, whilst reading them over the shoulder of Prior Gregory and knew the writing well. Isabella's large and clear; Susan's cramped, small, spidery and difficult to read.

How did they get there? I cannot recall picking them up just prior to waking. Now I am really scared. I am alone and insecure. Someone must have placed the diaries on my table, but who?

No point in sitting here worrying though, so I spent an hour scanning the diaries onto my computer and placing them at the bottom of my storage box for you, Suzanne. Anyone else would immediately jump to the conclusion that I was either totally out of my mind or that I was trying to concoct a mystery story. But you will believe me I know, although if you have some difficulty in doing so I quite understand. I am not sure I believe it myself!

Time for more regression I think. If I am to find out more about this weird regression thing, I <u>must</u> continue. So with much trepidation, I made myself comfortable on the bed this time, closed my eyes and started to count...three...

6

All through his babyhood, Sister Teresa dominated the child's life, providing care and love for the fractious, wilful Henri. By the time he attained his second birthday he was strutting about and issuing orders to the nuns as though he was master of their house. They all adored the robust intelligent boy and although Sister Teresa tried her best, he was spoiled. But all this time Mother Superior kept away from him, refusing to even acknowledge the presence of the son of a Romani person and allowing him to remain only because it was the wish of the Prior.

When Henri was just four years and three months old, Father Gregory entered his life as more than an occasional visitor and undertook his early education. This was not intended to occur for another two years but Sister Teresa met an untimely death.

Her body was discovered in the lake with the small Henri sitting athwart the overturned rowing boat in the lake, screaming his head off. He told his rescuers that they had been travelling to Elder Island to gather the elderflowers that blossomed in profusion at that time of year.

"The boat," he said, "just tipped when Sister Teresa turned to look over her shoulder to see how close we were to the island. We were thrown into the water and I managed to grab the boat then clamber onto it, but I couldn't see Sister Teresa anywhere so I yelled."

Everyone assumed that she was dragged down by the weight of her clothing and drowned and young Henri appeared to be distraught at the loss of his foster mother. The infant Henri could, however, have told them a different story.

He had played at the edges of the lake during summertime since he was able to walk and by the time he was three found he was able to support his own weight on the water by just lying supine. However, he kept this and his subsequent ability to swim from his guardian and during the trip to Elder Island with Sister Teresa, the small Henri apparently fell from the boat. Sister Teresa naturally attempted to rescue him but toppled over and found herself pulled down by the skirts of her habit. Unfortunately, her struggles did little to release the hold of an agile figure with the ability to hold his breath underwater, and the panic-stricken nun soon succumbed to the inhalation of sufficient lake waters to drown her.

Thus, it was that Henri was introduced to the brotherhood at an earlier than intended age.

~

By day he spent time under the tuition of Father Gregory and for exercise and outdoor activities Brother John took the young Henri under his wing. This was a good move as Brother John was by far the youngest of the monks and Henri liked him. He was agile enough to catch the child when he took it into his head to run off – not an irregular habit. However, despite his perverse behaviour the two grew fond of each other and became good friends. Brother John thought he taught Henri to swim, kicked a bladder with him, taught him the names of trees and plants, which of these were safe to eat and which were poisonous. These were the lessons the boy enjoyed. He also displayed a great ability to learn the names of the stars and to identify them, from the North Star to Orion's Belt. But Henri was less inclined to learn his letters and numbers, and it was this lack of attention that prompted Father Gregory to intervene for the purpose of teaching these important subjects to an unwilling pupil. He was a good teacher and had a way of making these subjects into an interesting story that grabbed the boy's attention and he soon proved an ability to absorb his lessons, despite himself.

Notwithstanding his naughtiness, Henri found it easy to appear to be a likeable little chap and soon became a firm favourite of all the Monks, who tended to spoil him and keep as much as possible of his misbehaviour from the Prior. He was allocated a small cell next to that of Brother John and from that time on saw very little of the Sisters who had previously cared for his welfare.

~

The Prior now assumed that he was the only person aware of Henri's true parentage and as to the best of his knowledge no further communication had been received from the Count, Father Gregory was content that the identity of his ward was safe.

However, Mother Superior at the Hospice of St Patrick's continued to keep in contact with her companions at the Convent of the Golden Orb in Switzerland, and she had reported her suspicions that the boy was not, in fact, a Romani child. After the death of Sister Teresa, Mother Superior felt that the boy was whisked away from the Sisters of Serenity with too much haste. She was of the opinion that Prior Gregory showed an inordinate interest in the child and recalled that Sister Serena had some time before, told her that he appeared to be able to swim, having seen him alone at the lake early one morning. At the time she had ignored it – she had no interest in a Romani child – but he had the looks of an aristocrat, not those of a Romani or peasant farm stock.

Thus, she reported this and the information was passed to the Count who was willing to wait for the right moment to contact his son. Meanwhile, he would be able to influence Henri through the means of occult magic.

The strange dreams, which he had started to experience, were difficult for such a young boy to understand, but gradually Henri began to put together the content and to believe that he was intended to act upon the information received. At first, the dreams were simply mischievous, but the young child soon realised that these visions would guide his life, alongside that received from the monks with whom he dwelt.

~

Michael had slotted a note in at this point.

~

It was at this point that I changed from the understanding that information regarding Henri was being filed into my brain. Changed from the person I am now but perfectly healthy, being present at the Priory as it was then, with the ability to observe but not be seen, to being in Henri and living with and through him.

To summarise:

- *The introduction to Prior Gregory and Sister Teresa.*
- *The birth of Henri De Ville.*
- *The story as told by Sister Teresa regarding Isabella de Ville.*
- *The reading of the diaries of Isabella and Susan regarding the Convent of the Golden Orb and the Count.*
- *Subsequent events at St Patrick's Priory following the birth of Henri De Ville.*
- *The death of Sister Teresa and the entry of Henri to the tuition of Prior Gregory and the monks.*

You will recall that I found the two diaries on my table. I am now able to confirm that they are still where I put them, in the box and have checked the memory sticks on which I scanned their contents. I think that if you were to check the age of the paper you will find they are dated circa eighteen/nineteen hundred.

How do I come to have them in my possession? I know not!

Anyway, what follows is in the first person, for that is how these latest experiences appear.

7

My inclinations were directed more to the strange teachings within my dreams, so I have to be very careful to maintain my Brother Henri persona. This does not seem very difficult though – perhaps the interesting Man in Black who appears to me in my visions is able to help me in this respect.

Father Gregory, who tells me Bible stories and the basic dictates of the Roman Catholic Church, primarily provides my religious instruction. I am not particularly interested but seem to have no need to pay much attention, as when required to do so I find I am able to quote from the Bible – chapter and verse – and to sing psalms in my sweet clear boy soprano voice. How I achieve these feats of memory I neither know nor care. From the age of five I am always obliged to attend the three services of Angelus at 6 am: noon and 6 pm: that commemorate the Annunciation, and invariably have to be dragged from my bed by Brother John in time to attend the 6 am: prayers. Mass, from which I am for the time being excluded, is said before the first Angelus, and after these prayers, we would break our fast. At noon I am usually kneeling in my place, the thoughts in my mind though are not on the prayers being recited, but on the meal that will follow. It isn't that I am unable to follow the words that commemorate the Annunciation but am simply indifferent to them. The 6 pm service also precedes our evening meal but by this time after an energetic day, I am getting tired and easily bored.

When I was eleven, being bored with this regular similarity, I brought a rat into the chapel. I had removed it from a nest before fur covered its tiny body, shutting the creature in a box I managed to acquire from Father Gregory's room, subsequently removing it therefrom and secreting it in the pocket of my robe. The box contained a valued Bible, given to the Prior by his parents when he entered the Church, the pages of which served well as bedding for my rat. In my dreams the previous night, I had learned what fun could be had with my pet. Father Gregory was droning on, the monks responding with their monotonous chant. Everyone was kneeling, hands clasped with foreheads resting upon them and eyes closed. Except me of course, kneeling in the centre of the fourth-row pew. Ratty was in my pocket, periodically nuzzling my hand with his soft nose.

Strange! I find I have given the creature a name. I am almost fond of him. This is not allowed. The rat was saved from the same fate as its siblings, merely because I had a use for it. I felt no recrimination at pulling the legs and tails from those horrid pink things or breaking the neck of their mother. On the contrary, I enjoyed their squeals and the angry cries of the mother as she watched twelve of her brood of thirteen, die in agony. I had trapped her under a sieve from the kitchen and she almost managed to escape by biting through the fine weave, but I was quick and a sharp blow across her nose stunned her until I was ready. I had hoped to inflict the same punishment upon the mother rat as her babies, but she was too strong for me to hold still, so her demise was speedy, as her neck broke under the blow from a rock.

These thoughts soon brought me back to the plan in hand, so glancing around to ensure no one had an eye on me, I silently ducked under the pew in front, turning left and crawling to the end, removing Ratty from my pocket as I did so.

Brother Caradoc comes from Wales and far from being a strong fighting Welshman, he is a tiny scraggy little fellow, frightened of his own shadow, with an unnatural fear of creeping insects and mice. Which was how I came to choose him as the recipient of Ratty. He was seated between Brothers Jean-Guy and Tubal at the far end, the tips of his large, grubby feet poking from beneath his brown robe. I subdued a giggle and the desire to tickle them, but instead gently lifted the robe and placed Ratty between his skinny legs. Then, without more ado backed with all speed to my place next to Brother John. I was kneeling in prayer just like everyone else when poor old Caradoc erupted from his place with a scream. The heavy pew toppled but was prevented from falling by the monks knelt before it. Father Prior ceased praying and stood aghast with hands spread before him as though to deter the sound of screams. Skinny little Caradoc twisted and turned, slapping at his body as poor Ratty darted about the squirming body. Finally, the monk threw himself down in the aisle and rolled. The rat darted from under the clothes that had trapped him and…ran straight to me.

I kept the creature imprisoned in the box without food for seven days then pinned it down by its feet and the base of its tail and slowly beat it to death.

Unfortunately, it died with the first blow, as at such a tender age I had not yet realised the effects of starvation on such a small body. Nevertheless, I enjoyed the process and it did help to atone for the beating I received for my prank. However, as it was my friend Brother John who was chosen to administer the whipping, it was applied half-heartedly, and unlike Brother Caradoc, I held my silence. In fact, I refused to speak to anyone at all for the next three weeks.

I did other things during the next three years but made sure I was not caught out again by a mere animal that appeared to think I was its pack leader.

It was after the above episode that Father Gregory decreed that I move to the room above his own in the tower. This pleased me greatly as I had no difficulty in scrambling down the ivy-covered sides, something I did regularly at night. I became skilled at telling myself how long I wished to sleep and invariably awoke just after midnight when the Prior was snoring peacefully in his bed. I knew this, not because the sound was audible through the floor, on the contrary with doors firmly closed the rooms were soundproof, but because I would sometimes enter the old man's room and stand by his bed. He never knew this, of course, and would have undoubtedly, been perturbed by it had he done so.

By the time I was fourteen years of age, I began collecting henbane, laurel, laburnum and other poisonous plants that I secreted in my room under the base of my closet, which I had prised loose. To start with, I was not sure why I did this, but then the dreams began to make clear the purpose and how I was supposed to proceed.

Ah! The bells are ringing…

~

Ringing…ringing…

I awoke with a start. A bell was ringing. Then I realised it was the front doorbell. I was confused between the bell of St Patrick's Priory, what should be my alarm clock and what was actually the doorbell.

Damn! I had to answer it because if it were one of Helena Rose's arrangements with Dr Richard or one of our neighbours, they would phone her if they got no response. Fortunately, they would not expect me to get there very quickly, so I had no need to hasten. The bell rang again – better get a move on!

The clock informed me that only half my allotted time of three hours had passed. The bell rang once again.

"Okay! I'm coming as fast as I can," I yelled.

"Hello Mike, how are you? I was getting worried."

It was you, Suzanne. I remembered now that I had left a message on your voicemail to tell you that Helena Rose was away for a couple of days, and bless you, you did what I hoped, came to visit me.

I led the way through to the kitchen and asked if you wanted tea or coffee. But once in the kitchen, you insisted that I sit whilst you made tea. "I assume everything is still in the same place?" you asked.

I said, "Sure. Biscuits are now in that tub thing with a clown head though, and no, they don't keep as fresh as they did in the fridge. Anyway, I don't eat that much these days."

You raised your eyebrows in that way you have as you placed a mug of tea in front of me. You sensed all was not as well as it might be and I guess I should be grateful that after all I had put you through, you are still willing to give me support, albeit somewhat undercover.

We chatted amicably enough for fifteen minutes or so, and it was during that time I decided on my next action.

I didn't go into deep detail but told you how I had visited Dr Jennings all those years ago and the effect that thinking or dreaming about that time had on me. I explained about Peter de Ville and Jamie Cameron too but again didn't go into much detail. Then I told you how I have been recording on computer discs and cassettes, explaining how I intend to seal them in a secure box for your eyes only.

"I can't leave my notes for Helena Rose, she'd either burn them or sell them to some tacky newspaper. Once that happens, I would be a nine-day wonder nutcase, and she'll be rich. Suzanne, I need you to put the whole thing together, and if necessary after I pop my clogs, to seek out the Man in Black/the Count or whoever that evil character might be, and destroy him."

"What haven't you told me Mike?" you said.

"Okay. Yes, there is more, it's Henri de Ville. He was way back farther than the others and lives in a monastery. He's bad – very bad. I haven't come to the end of his time yet but I do believe that I am a reincarnation of those three characters and it must stop. I don't have much longer now, maybe six months but that will be enough time to complete my notes. If she doesn't offer you the box then you must ask Helena Rose for it. The fact that you know just where it is should help, but don't tell her what is in it, make some excuse, old articles, containing your photos or whatever."

"Oh Michael, you know I will do as you ask if I can, but how on earth am I to locate this man?"

"You won't need to, Suzanne, you will have all the relevant documents – he will find you, my dear. I am so sorry. This may put you in terrible danger, my true love. You don't have to accept it if you don't want to, it's just the only thing I can think of to close the circle of evil."

You got that puzzled look on your face again, then…

"I accept your challenge, after all, I am supposed to be an investigative journalist, so if anyone should be able to sort it then that person is me."

"You are so faithful a friend, my Suzanne, so strong, brave, tenacious, but what is that fiend you will need to deal with on your own? What danger have I now put in your way?"

No! I must change my mind. I cannot allow you to risk your precious life.

But you said, "Too late Mike. You know very well that I can't refuse a challenge. I shall be all of a twitter until I get my hands on that Pandora's box of yours. Now, is there anything I can bring you before her ladyship returns?"

I assured you that I had all I needed and after you had washed our mugs and made sure I was comfortable; we said our goodbyes and parted. I had a gut feeling that this was the last time we would meet and fought back the threatening tears until you left, then flopped onto the bed and gave way to despair. I must have sobbed myself to sleep, for when I next woke up it was already dark. I struggled to the bathroom and splashed cold water over my head, then feeling fresher made my way to the kitchen and shoved a ready meal into the microwave. I ate the meal – can't remember what it was – then sat with a cup of coffee, going over what had happened at the Priory of St Patrick's. It occurred to me that I had been in the head of Henri, not reading notes over the shoulder of the Prior, so I inserted a few notes for you before adding Henri's Ratty prank.

I am trying to eliminate confusion but can't help thinking I might be adding to it!

I was aching from pillar to post by now, so I took a couple of painkillers and retreated to my bed, feeling sorry for myself. However, I was aware by now that there was no certainty whether I would sleep or regress, so setting the alarm for three hours and the recorder to voice motivation, I eased myself into a comfortable position and closed my eyes. I must have drifted off, for the next thing I knew was…

8

Over the next several months, I acquired knowledge of the capabilities of the poisonous plants in my possession with the assistance of the Priory cats, kept for the purpose of catching mice and rats. I ascertained the amounts and types required to make them very ill, to render them unconscious for long periods of time, and to cause death. But it is one thing to experiment on animals, quite another to ascertain what effect these might have on a man, and in this case, I cannot take any unnecessary risks. I must get it right the first time.

Hence, for the next few weeks, I must make myself helpful and pleasant to not only the monks but especially to Father Gregory. There is more than one reason for this. I need to learn some pretty serious mathematics concerning quantities, weights etc., to draw myself closer to the Prior on a personal level, and by my very solicitude reduce his concentration of my own activities. I was diligent and industrious in my studies; I attended even more services than required of me and at the age of fourteen, Father Gregory began to school me for confirmation into the Church. Every morning for the next two weeks, I arose earlier than the Prior and joined the other two postulant Brothers to help prepare for Mass and learn what will subsequently become my daily task. Father Gregory was delighted with me as I learned my catechism and showed readiness to become a postulant and subsequently enter the Priory as a monk.

I must act soon or shall find myself more deeply entrenched in this religious nonsense.

~

To get to the accommodation in the tower, it is necessary to climb a spiral stairway. This is made of granite slabs of about fifteen inches wide and twelve inches high. They are all worn down in a dip at the front centre by regular use and it pays to take care when ascending or descending as if one's footwear is wet the steps are slippery. Which is how the Prior came to meet an early death.

What a commotion!

When the Prior failed to show up in time for Mass, a thing that just never happened, he was a meticulous keeper of time, particularly where religious ceremonies are concerned, I was sent to see if he was perhaps ill. Of course, I knew that he was in fact beyond illness, but I raced to the tower where I once again checked that I had covered all the potentials. The top step had dried where I had scrubbed the grease from it, the spilt water in Father Gregory's room was still damp, but the soles of his sandals were now dry. Arranging my face into a shocked expression I ran back to the chapel, a saddened 14-year-old boy who had lost the man who had been guardian and father to him.

"He…he's dead!" I sobbed, running into the arms of Brother John.

"He's at the bottom of the stairs and his neck's all twisted."

That got them moving. Mass was forgotten as everyone made their way to the tower. The rest of the day was one of confusion, as preparation was made for the funeral.

I hovered around the brothers as they washed and dressed the broken body of the late Father Prior, making sure I got in the way consistently and sobbing broken-heartedly. Salt rubbed in my eyes gave the swollen redness, it jolly well hurt but was effective in that it produced the required saddened face of a bereaved young boy.

The burial service was a melancholy occurrence for the old Prior was well-loved. He was laid to rest in the cemetery, within the grounds of St Patrick's alongside others of his kind, and above the graves of the nuns, the latest one buried there being Sister Teresa. All those old nuns seemed to be at least a hundred years old to me, but although they appeared very old, they were also very tough.

~

I awoke in a slather of perspiration, my heart beating nineteen to the dozen. I was still within my dream, regression, or whatever it might have been, and found it difficult to regain reality.

I forced myself to lie still and count slowly to a hundred, by which time I had somewhat recovered my composure.

With difficulty, I eased myself from the bed and grabbing the walking frame I am now obliged to use, staggered into the shower and allowed the stinging shards of cold water to drench me until I shivered. Then I relaxed in a gentler spray of warm water and turning off the water donned my towelling gown.

In the kitchen I boiled the kettle, made a chiffonier of coffee and nearly burnt some toast; that is what happens when I work on automatic pilot. It was only just seven o'clock but the paper had been delivered and I must confess I enjoyed the unusually early breakfast all by myself. Radio Three was playing Haydn's Concerto for Oboe and Orchestra in C Minor and I felt more relaxed than I have done for ages.

I must have sat there for an hour or more, but eventually, I realised that as I was feeling more robust, I had better put the time to good use and get what happened during the night, onto my computer.

~

This task being completed and it being 12.30 pm. I made some tea and a cheese sandwich (sliced bread and ready sliced cheese I fear) to which I added a good dollop of tomato pickle as this stuff doesn't have much taste.

Now I shall save what I have written and shut this machine down, then relax on the recliner and see what happens next!

Part II
Henri De Ville

9

It was nearly six months later towards the end of May that our new Prior joined us.

Brother Jeane-Paul came from France, although to judge by his spoken English, had been raised in this country. He was rather effeminate, with small features, thin blond hair, ice-blue eyes and elegant hands. He was no more than five feet four inches tall and his voice was soft, with the emphasis rising at the end of a sentence. Prior Jeane-Paul as he was now, soon became addressed amongst the monks as Father Jeane-Paul, having quickly become a popular figure at St Patrick's. He was not at all like Father Gregory with his deep intellect, serious demeanour and all-encompassing faith. Jeane-Paul was a man of the people with the ability to preach a sermon that was understandable to them – and me.

I made it my business to be solicitous and ensured that he believed I looked up to him as my mentor, studied hard and was confirmed into the Church. In which ceremony I kept my fingers crossed and silently revoked each sentence after I spoke it.

By the time I was fifteen, I had shown an affinity for the art of illuminated scrolls and calligraphy. This skill was encouraged and Father Jeane-Paul seemed to like my company, often sitting with me, his arm flung loosely around my shoulders. Young as I was, he would talk to me for hours on end, which was how I learnt of his history in France.

Apparently, he had belonged to a monastery high in the French Alps, having been incarcerated there by his family when they discovered his proclivity for men rather than women. After many years, he had fallen in love with a monk, one Brother Julien who had transferred from America, and they had indulged in a surreptitious relationship. Someone had apparently learned of this clandestine relationship and threatened to tell the Abbot. However, before this could happen Father Jeane-Paul's friend hanged himself. Which is how when Jeane-Paul learned there was a position as Prior at St Patrick's, he implored his Abbot to set in motion the request for transfer. Now I know what his interest in me is about and promptly made sure he never got the opportunity of spending much time alone in my company.

Thus, I made sure I was left pretty much to myself at the top of the tower. I achieved this largely solitary existence by throwing a tantrum if anyone tried to visit my room without having arranged to do so beforehand. For the next year, I still attended services and studies but gradually allowed these to cease in such a manner that it was not noticed. Meals, of course, were still eaten in the refectory, and liking my food at regular times I made sure that I was at my place, hands in lap, eyes and head lowered in a reverent manner.

Also, I provided samples of my art and calligraphy on a regular basis to the Prior, who subsequently drooled over it with his favoured group of Brothers. Meanwhile, I quietly returned to my room and wedged a chair under the latch to prevent the unwanted entry of visitors.

By this time, I was speedily approaching my sixteenth birthday and the dreams I had previously experienced, returned. These were not the same as before but instructed me as to my future behaviour. So it was that the reasons for climbing through my window and down the ivy were changed. Freedom was achieved. I removed my habit and clad in clothes acquired by stealth from a market held weekly in our village, I would make my way to the local hostelry.

The Dog and Duck is a cosy place, with huge oak beams supporting a thatched roof and thick planks forming a ceiling. At one end is a fireplace stacked with logs, though at this time of year no fire is necessary. Mine host George Marlow, a small skinny man with sharp features, his stringy hair tied back at his scraggy neck, attended the bar at the opposite end of the building. Mrs Marlow is the reverse of her husband. She is a very large woman, having arms and legs like those of a blacksmith. Her complexion is flawless but overly ruddy in hue, and there is no doubt as to which of them rules the roost at the Dog and Duck. On the other hand, their daughter seems to belong to some other couple, but perhaps it is that she has inherited the best of both parents, having her mother's flawless complexion, h in her case is pure English roses. She is small and slim like her father, her eyes are clear blue, her mouth a perfect bow waiting to be kissed and her hair is a mass of shining blond waves that cascade over her shoulders. She does not serve behind the bar and is only seen when the hostelry is very busy when she is required to collect and wash the tankards. I desire her.

But it was not the beautiful Maggie who provided my first experience. No, it was her mother, the buxom Bessie. Probably a good thing on reflection, as Maggie is probably as much a virgin as I.

To achieve my required pleasures, I made sure that I gradually become a well-known face in the Dog and Duck over the past month. The regulars think I am employed on a temporary basis to make general small repairs and do gardening jobs at the Priory, and for which I receive lodgings. They are merely serfs, of course, with no ability to read or write. If they possessed a brain larger in size than that of a pea, they would know the Monks get to do all the little jobs themselves. However, it suffices to cover the fact that I always arrive from the direction of the Priory and that I am generally unknown in the village.

But beer has to be paid for. Monks give up all their rights to personal wealth so it is necessary for me to obtain it by other means. A process that has proved much easier than I at first envisaged. In the beginning, I helped myself from the cash box held by the Priory Treasurer, Brother Ananias, but it is necessary to be careful and I want, need, more. He's a doddery old fool but not stupid, so any large discrepancy would be noticed. However, I have ensured that the Brother Treasurer thinks of me as a young man after his own heart, with an interest and quickness for numbers. I very kindly offered my services as scribe to him, for which he is most grateful, as his sight is somewhat impaired, and which enables me to be somewhat creative with his particular numbers.

Maggie had been collecting tankards and I engaged her in conversation, during which I endeavoured to fondle her posterior. She squealed and retreated to the kitchen, where after a while I followed. To my surprise, Maggie was not there – but Buxom Bessie was. She took me by the hand and led me outside to the barn. There she stroked me, bringing me speedily to an orgasm. But Buxom Bertha did not stop there, she spoke quietly and showed me what is required by a woman whilst indulging in the sexual act. Then grasping my testicles firmly in her large hand she squeezed until I begged for mercy.

"If you touch my daughter again," she said, "I will castrate you."

And with no more ado, she left me. I have not shown my face at the Dog and Duck since. I learned my lessons – all of them – but must look elsewhere to indulge my pleasures.

For the next six months, I did not leave the sanctuary of the Priory, still helping Brother Treasurer and acquiring quite a useful store of cash for myself. This I hid under a loose floorboard beneath my bed in the tower. In fact, I placed it in the box in which Ratty had once been incarcerated and which since that time had held all my collections, whether it be poisonous plants, insects or money.

~

The dreams had diminished in their intensity during what I think of as my quiet time. I wrote, embroidered my illuminated scrolls, and ensured they were handed to Brother John, ate my evening meal in the refectory with the Monks and attended enough services to fool the Brothers that I was one of them. I arranged to place myself in a position beside a pillar, where if I chose not to attend others would assume they had missed seeing me, but not that I was absent. I became pretty good at this deception too.

I was a bored young man – well getting on for sixteen. My desires had certainly not decreased and Maggie's body was the only one worth thinking about when I masturbated. All right, as a Monk, I was not supposed to have such thoughts and certainly not such actions, but I am not a man to deny myself pleasures of any variety.

~

On the eve of my sixteenth birthday, I entered my room at the top of the tower to find a man dressed in the black garb of a priest sitting at my table. Had it been the Prior, or one of the Brothers, I would have been very angry, but my only perception was one of curiosity. I recognised him as the man who appeared in my dreams.

"Who are you, what do you want of me?"

His reply somewhat staggered me, for he said, "I am your father."

"But both my parents are dead, my mother at my birthing and my father…"

…I realised that no one had ever mentioned my father – I knew nothing whatsoever about him.

The man purporting to be my father smiled. A tight up turning of his narrow lips with no mirth lighting his cold ice-blue eyes and at that moment I felt a frisson of chill to my very bones. Those eyes drew me in, taking from me my willpower, as I sat on the floor at his bidding, never releasing my gaze from his. He seemed not to speak but nevertheless, knowledge of my conception and birth infiltrated, knowledge taking their place in a head that was no longer mine to control.

As his tale reached the present, I felt a return of my persona, slowly, gradually I was able to take in what was being said in a normal manner. Excitement took over from trepidation and I was ready to listen to anything and everything this man had to tell me.

He promised to introduce me to friends at the Manor House and encouraged all my desires. Then placing his slim long-fingered hand on my head, he blessed me in a manner I had certainly never heard within the confines of the Priory, exalting one he called The Master of Mankind and entreating him to keep me within the Circle of the Golden Orb. Then he was no longer there.

I sat on the floor where I had been directed for a long time, trying to get what had happened clear in my head. I cannot remember his departure. Certainly, there were no farewells or any indication that he would visit me again at any time. However, I knew in my mind that he would be waiting in my tower room when the time was right and was quite content with that. My father! The man is my father! I had not asked his name but somehow knew to refer to him as Papa Count. I knew I was special, but for the moment could not recall the details. Never mind, they are safe in my head and will be remembered when I need them. For the moment, the bell is ringing for the six o'clock Angelus and it is essential that I do not vary my behaviour for the time being.

~

The alarm woke me three hours later, blending with the Angelus bell at St Patrick's Priory. I was stiff, not having moved my position for some time and it took me a while to come around sufficiently to be able to stand. Then I staggered to the kitchen. The stupid cow-shaped clock informed me that it was now 6.30 pm and the sky was covered with dark clouds. In the distance, I could hear a rumble of thunder. I watched for the next flash of lightning and counted ten before the following clap of thunder. About ten miles away I calculated and drawing closer by the minute. I filled the kettle, set it to boil, inserted some toast under the grill and some baked beans (already placed in a glass dish by Helena Rose for my convenience) in the microwave. I even remembered to pierce the plastic film!

The reason for this unaccustomed speed and lack of proper preparation of my usual dinner was due to the fact that in this area we frequently suffer electricity cuts during a storm. I jumped as the lightning was followed instantly by a clap of thunder immediately overhead. The storm was all around the area now, flash, zigzag, flash; it was reminiscent of my experiences in the 1914/18 war, as Peter de Ville, with the flashes of fire and ear-splitting noise of guns. Strange! I find myself thinking of that experience as an actual memory rather than a regression.

Suzanne, I worry about my sanity but will nevertheless continue this narrative.

The electric cables somehow managed to avoid a lightning strike this time so I could have had a proper meal – never mind I don't often get to eat what Helena Rose describes as lower-class fast food. Perhaps I'll get Suzanne to bring me some good old-fashioned fish and chips. Do they still wrap them in newspapers? I doubt it, they probably come in small plastic boxes. Something else to add to the piles of non-biodegradable rubbish!

By the way, I dictated this onto my digital recorder after eating my fill. The storm had abated, the static electricity that raises all the small hairs on my arms and legs having disappeared with a hailstorm that left piles of frozen ice balls. The hail has now turned to a steady rain, which periodically bursts into that hard stair-rod type of rain that lasts only for perhaps thirty seconds, then slows down for five or ten minutes, only to try for another spurt.

When I listen to what I have said, it seems as though someone is reading a story, recorded from the radio. What I am trying to say is that the fluency surprises me. If I tried to relay a normal dream in this way it would just not happen in the same manner, for when remembering a dream, the details are there but not the emotions. My memory of these proceedings is the same as when it happened in the regression. It is this that makes me feel a confirmation that these regressions are indeed memories of previous lives as lived by yours truly.

It is now nine o'clock and I am tired, so God Bless you, Suzanne.

I have to be careful how I spend my time tomorrow, for I am not sure whether Helena Rose will be home Friday evening or early Saturday morning. I must have a note somewhere, she always leaves notes, obviously thinks I am not sensible enough to remember what she would consider important. God! She would have me put away if she discovered and read these notes!

GOOD NIGHT!

~

I had one of the best night's sleep for some weeks. Obviously, the baked beans did not have an adverse effect on me. Perhaps it was because I felt more relaxed, being on my own in the house. Am I afraid that my wife might smother me in the night? No, I think not. Her way would be through drugs of some description, she knows so much about them and probably is aware of the ones that would not leave a signature. But there is no need for her to do that either. Why risk a possible murder charge when the one you need rid of is on the way out of his own accord?

Anyway, I can't say that I leapt from my bed, but did manage to exit it without too much hassle.

I'd just completed my morning ablutions and managed to pull on my clothes when the phone rang. Damn! At this time, it could only be Helena Rose. "Deville Speaks," I roared, knowing quite well that it would infuriate her and make her ears ring. Having assured her that I am managing very well all by myself, that I slept, and am eating properly (didn't mention last night's dinner) she was persuaded to go about her own business. She will be home about seven – botheration. I wonder how I will sleep tonight.

Breakfast completed with only a quick glance at the paper, I am back in my recliner, speaking into the recording machine and preparing to regress. It's a pretty easy thing to accomplish now, so here goes…

10

I have started dreaming again but this time I am being shown how to play certain games of cards. At the moment I am not aware of their names, but I am a quick learner and it behoves me to learn the precepts of the game. By the end of the week, I have learnt, in my sleep, how to play three complicated games that I understand are an indulgence of the aristocracy. These night-time studies seem to tire me more than usual dreaming and I can only assume that is because my brain is fully active, storing the information. Consequently, I overslept on four out of the seven days, thereby missing early Mass. Father Prior called me to his room and I received a severe lashing of his tongue concerning my tardy behaviour. I did what was expected of me, hung my head, apologised profusely and made sure I stirred my bones early for the next three days. The only way I could achieve this was to get my friend Brother John to wake me.

Learning the card games was interesting but the next step far exceeded that experience. I was taught how to cheat during the games, thereby accumulating winnings. This excited me, for I knew Papa Count was influencing these dreams for a purpose. So it was no surprise to find a pack of cards wrapped in my habit on the third day. I had been shown how to cheat, now it was my job to practice the sleight of hand required to do this effectively.

Incidentally, I was delighted to find my tiredness had dispersed and was once again waking automatically at five o'clock each day. Brother John still banged on my door each morning, until I advised him that my malady had apparently been cured, to which news he praised God and pointed out the answering of the prayers of righteous men.

My comments would not have been reverent or polite and I have learnt to hold my peace!

Then the training dreams ceased and I knew that I must now perfect my skills. It took me three full weeks of constant practice before I was able to manipulate the cards so that it was impossible for another to see what I was up to. I then confirmed my skill by showing off some simple sleight-of-hand tricks to the brothers during our communal hours. Some, like Brother John, were much impressed by my magic but the older monks muttered amongst themselves that such things were of the devil, and thus tried to discourage me.

The next day, I showed them how it was that I performed a certain trick, assuring them that was all it entailed. They still disapproved of my conjuring but for the most accepted that my tricks were just that, tricks.

Phew! That was a close shave. I knew how nearly they had reported me to the Prior and only the younger monks had persuaded them to give me a chance to explain. Brother John warned me, so I was prepared and my dream that night had shown me the way.

Returning to my cell following Vespers one night, nearly a year after his first visit, I found my father, Papa Count, sitting on my bed. My heart jumped and I felt excitement tinged with both fear and joy, for surely the next stage of my young life was about to be set in motion…

~

I am both excited by what I am discovering and afraid of what I will assuredly learn. There is no doubt in my mind now that I have been regressing over previous lives; and perhaps the Man in Black, Dracula or Henri's father, Papa Count, by whatever name you choose to acknowledge this evil character, will reveal to me what I might expect in my future life. I suspect the latter will only cover the next task he has in mind for me. It is too much to hope he might reveal the reason for my subsequent lives up to the twenty-first century.

I have a feeling, Suzanne, of being drained of all energy once I am back in the reality of this world. It is a frightening experience and sometimes I wonder whether I will not in fact return but find myself in the eighteenth century forever. If that should happen, will someone find my twenty-first century body or will Michael Deville just disappear from the face of the earth? However, I am sure The Count will not allow my release until he is ready to relax his hold on my life.

Could this be a parallel world where time works in reverse rather than forward as we know it? But to dwell on those thoughts is a path to madness.

I should get something to eat as if another regression is to be completed before Helena Rose returns I need to replenish my energy, for no doubt much will be taken during that period.

During my time in the body of Henri de Ville, I not only lose energy but feel that my very soul is depleted each time I listen to Papa Count.

Suzanne, dear Suzanne, you are reading and listening to these notes so obviously, I am no longer living in your world. That may not mean that my essence is not still around and should that be the case I promise to protect you to the best of my ability. But watch carefully and take great care, for the Man in Black will always be around somewhere, causing chaos wherever and whenever he can.

~

11

I was just coming up to my eighteenth birthday and becoming seriously bored with my existence in the Monastery when Papa Count once again appeared in my room.

He was in his usual black and red attire but this time was also wearing a large, reversed cross, in dark jade. He greeted me, holding it away from himself, still in the upside-down position, saying.

"May our Master Greet and Guide you my son."

He then told me to prepare to leave the Monastery within a few days when I was to be taken to the City of London to ply my trade as a street Magician. I would learn more in due course. Then he bade me to kneel, close my eyes and kiss his cross. Upon opening my eyes again, with the feeling of that object still upon my lips, he had disappeared.

It was on the night of the fourth day that through a dream I was summoned to depart, so gathering together the things I had stashed in a canvas bag, I climbed from my window down the ivy for the last time. A coach and horses were waiting on the far side of the wall and the journey to London began. The coach contained only myself and the driver, who only spoke to enquire if I was to be his passenger. It was a long and uncomfortable journey but in a state of expectation, I felt only excitement. We travelled through the rest of that night and the next day, stopping at Inns to refresh ourselves and replace the horses. I saw the driver as I disembarked and re-entered the coach but had no further conversation with him. When arriving in London, he stopped at my lodgings and without further ado, drove off again.

My lodgings were more than adequate and considering I had been residing in a monastery for the whole of my life could be called luxurious. They were in a large house that apparently provided rooms for such as travellers and students. The rooms contained a bed with a more comfortable mattress than that to which I was accustomed, filled, as I later discovered, with duck feathers. *I wonder if*

Maggie of the Dog & Duck has such comfort. I was also given two warm blankets and feeling tired and somewhat battered from my journey, I threw myself into the comfort of the bed and fell immediately to sleep.

When I awoke, it was daylight and the chiming of a clock told me it was five o'clock in the afternoon. I suppose I must have slept for twelve or more hours.

Having heard nothing more from Papa Count, I spent the next week exploring the vast city, allowing my feet to carry me where they would. I discovered St Paul's Cathedral with its amazing dome of glass. Having known no church building but St Patrick's, this immense structure of such beauty took my breath away. It was not until I had finally walked away from that particular area that my mind once again turned to the task at hand. I was not expecting such feelings and that experience would in the future focus me towards another path.

~

During my walks, I found places where street markets were established; exactly the area for yours truly to set up a stall. So it was that the following morning I arrived at the first of my choice and placing a small folding table before me, prepared to fleece the gathering crowd. At its feet was a board painted red and on which was printed in gold lettering, the words:

THE GREAT MAGICIAN OF THE GOLDEN ORB

I was wearing a garment over my customary apparel that I found in the cupboard of my room. It was a bright red robe trimmed with gold braid, with wide pointed sleeves and reaching to my feet. On my head, I wore a similarly coloured and decorated beret, which pulled down and covered the tips of my ears.

I soon learned that to ply my trade I was obliged to voice it loud enough to be heard above those other stallholders, who indeed had longer experience of this than I did. However, I had the advantage of being a newcomer and thus drew the interest of potential purchasers of whatever a Magician might have to offer. I lured the first by asking him to withdraw any card from my proffered pack, to check what it was without allowing me to see and to return the same anywhere into the pack. This he did, upon which I told him he had chosen the Queen of Hearts. It was, of course, correct and served to encourage further interest. But I was there to take their money, not to perform for their entertainment. So it was I asked the gentleman if he wished to indulge in another type of magic. He was willing, so it was agreed that for the price of two farthings, he placed a shilling coin under a cup, of which there were three. I then moved them back and forth to cause confusion and asked him to say under which cup the coin resided, if he was correct the original plus one other shilling would be his, if on the other hand, he was not correct then the original shilling coin would be mine. He did of course lose and I pocketed the coin. Naturally, the gentleman was determined to win back his coin so repeated the game and this time I allowed him to win. This, of course, proved to him that it certainly was possible to win, so tried again but this time I retrieved the coin. Which encouraged him to try again and once again he lost. After another half dozen losses, the gentleman chose to let someone else try against my magic and by the end of the day; I had collected some fifteen silver shillings and forty-five farthings. I proved that to let a person win occasionally, served to bring in more people with a gambling instinct, wishing to pit their abilities against those of the Great Magician.

By the end of the first month, I had accrued quite a small fortune and was beginning to be well known at several street markets. I was also becoming known to those who would prefer to get me off the streets altogether and was obliged to move my lodgings in an effort to temporarily disappear.

However, it was shortly after that rather worrying time that Papa Count once again appeared in my life and I learnt that my next adventure was to take me to Switzerland, to the very place of my conception, the Convent of the Golden Orb. So it was that one week later, I boarded a ship which took me to France and from there by coach and horses to Switzerland. At the convent I was given a bed in the quarters of Papa Count and slept, exhausted by my journey, for a full thirty-six hours. When I awoke the sun was setting and the bells for Vespers rang their familiar sounds.

~

Damn! My alarm has just awoken me and dragged my body back to this century once more. I've been doing conjuring tricks in London, my fingers operating with dexterity, my body twisting and bending without pain and my legs taking me wherever I will. Now I have to gingerly drag myself to an upright position in an effort to get into the wheelchair.

At least I see that my recorder has operated throughout and appears to have moved with me through the time zone. That is a great relief as I am no longer obliged to remember what has happened and repeat it aloud. Technology is at an incredible state of innovation, it appears to develop further from month to month. Perhaps, in time, there will be a machine that after recording will, upon request, type the content onto a computer, or even a telephone receiver.

Henri heard the bells for vespers at the Convent of the Golden Orb, so I guess it must be evening and Helena Rose will be home soon. I had better look to tidying myself up a bit and move to the sitting room to await her. I no longer attempt to prepare or cook our evening meal as I used to do but sit with a book and allow her the pleasure of waiting on me.

I can hardly wait to regress, not only to find out what Henri's next task will be but to escape this constant and growing discomfort once again.

Another dreary meal is over and I am free to return to my bed. I shall turn on the television and either watch if there is anything worth watching or doze to yet another rerun. Whatever; I am going to take a sleeping tablet. They are strong enough, when taken with a couple of painkillers, to give me five or six hours of complete rest. Helena Rose will turn the television off before she goes to bed. Given her due, she does try her best to care for me, even though, I must confess, there is little reward and I suspect hope of my demise is never far from her thoughts. For which, in all due honesty, I cannot blame her.

12

When I awoke Papa Count was sitting on the chair next to my bed and opening my eyes I first registered the red, like blood, of his collar of divinity and then intense black. I quickly sat upright and swung my legs over the side of the bed, saying as politely as possible.

"Good morning, Papa Count."

"So, you have at last come to your senses, my son."

No response I felt was necessary, so I maintained silence and an expressionless face. I had learnt much on those market stalls, the main one being the ability to obscure my facial expressions and thus inner feelings from those around me. My father did not seem impressed by this skill and for the first time, gave me knowledge of a strength of which I was unaware. However, I also knew what his ability with the occult could achieve and had no inclination to be on the receiving end. So instead, I showed compliance and asked permission to make myself more suitable for his illustrious presence. This he graciously permitted and said he would return within one-half hour.

Precisely upon that time, I awaited Papa Count sitting at the table, where he joined me. A Nun entered laden with a tray containing my breakfast and a jug of hot beverage, of which my father instructed me to partake. After this, I felt much stronger and sat back to listen to what my next task would be.

With no preamble, Papa Count began…

"In the range of hills above the Convent of the Golden Orb is a cliff, below which is a ledge and at the back of it is a hidden cave. This cave leads down to the edge of a farm owned by Farmer Gelberger. This is the route your *Mother* used to escape through, with the help of her former governess and the Gelberger family."

The mention of my mother was said with such hatred and disdain that I had difficulty controlling my expression.

"This family," he continued, "still owns the farm, although it is now mostly run by the son, one Joshua Gelberger and his wife Susan, the former governess. They are a religious family of great prestige within the village of Billenbach, do-gooders."

This information was again said with disdain.

"Your task, my son, is to destroy that family in its entirety, so avenging the fact of my great achievement. Your being born in another country and attempting to keep you from my knowledge served to make the fulfilment of the prophecy after so many aeons, null and void, and my own life became as an actor rather than a benefactor within this world. However, by the guidance of The Master, nothing can be hidden from me within the Convent of the Golden Orb."

"How am I to achieve the destruction of a whole family Papa Count?" I asked, with as much interest in my tone as I could muster, when all I felt in truth was shock and disgust.

"Any way in which you can, my son. There are six members of the family now, Farmer Gelberger, his wife Hannah and son Joshua who, being married to Susan Blessed, have twin children, Isabella and Johannes."

"Can you not achieve this through your occult knowledge, Papa Count?" I asked.

At this, he turned to me in anger, saying.

"If this was a possibility, do you not think I would have done it years ago? Are you a fool? Through the prophecy, the birth child has to be taught by his father, which you may have noticed I have been doing since your early years. With that tuition I have been passing to my son, the powers given me when I was first born, having been conceived in the same manner as yourself. The mother's life is always terminated. The father's job is to pass his knowledge to his son, who will then succeed to the position of future Controller of the Prophecy. Unfortunately, things went wrong when Susan Blessed became involved. Because you were born, not only in another country but also in the confines of a Monastery, although I am able to pass my knowledge to you, it cannot be absorbed in its entirety so long as those who were involved in that circumstance are all still living. They must be removed from this earth to hell."

"You very adroitly dealt with those within the Convent and Monastery but the family *must* be dispatched so that you can become The Count and Controller of the Prophecy within the Convent of the Golden Orb."

"You will no doubt be able to think of some way to rid us of these unnecessary humans."

"You will go to the farm the same way you did whilst still in that woman's stomach, that is of the utmost importance. I would suggest that you plan your arrival after dark and burn them in their beds, one and all. The farmhouse has a thatched roof so should burn readily."

"Be ready tomorrow night."

With that announcement, he rose from the table and was gone.

I was very discomfited by this revelation and found that at the very top of my memories was that of St Paul's Cathedral and the feelings I received therein. My choices now were God or Satan. My fears now were God, Papa Count, or maybe myself, Henri de Ville.

~

On the following night, I was ready to climb to the same clifftop that my mother had reached nearly twenty years ago. I had no one to guide me but the instructions fed to me during the climb by Papa Count. This made it surprisingly easy. Equally so, the scramble down the cliff to the ledge and so into the cave to begin my descent. Just inside the cave entrance, I found a sturdy branch wrapped in cloth, together with a box of matches. Good, at least I should be able to see my way.

Within this cavern, I found I could receive no further guidance from my father, so it was with some trepidation that I carefully followed the indistinct pathway to the most beautiful cavern. It reminded me of St Pauls in its grandeur and once again I felt something of the God of Father Gregory. Perhaps the old Prior of St Patrick's was looking down at me. What on earth would that good man think of Brother Henri now? I felt shame as I saw the ethereal beauty of glistening stalactites and stalagmites. But now there were streams, some I could easily jump but some it was necessary to wade through and I was wet and very cold by now. There were also waterfalls. I finally came to one that had to be crab-walked behind, there was just a narrow, slippery ledge to traverse. So I said a prayer to God and an apology to Father Gregory, who had been a real father to me throughout my childhood, then stepped onto the ledge. It was indeed slippery…and…

~

His wife found Michael with a box clasped firmly to him. She closed his eyes but the box, which proved to be addressed to his ex-wife Suzanne, was removed by an employee of the local undertaker, as rigour mortis had set in.

One thing Helena Rose would never forget was the stark fear in Michael's eyes before she closed them. It was assumed that his mouth had fallen open as he passed from this world to the next but Helena Rose knew that it was a scream of terror.

Suzanne's Notes

Wow! Suzanne sat staring at the trees in her orchard, trying to get her thoughts together. She had researched Michael's box of information as she went, trying to confirm certain things that appeared to be impossible. The results had proved to be surprising and at the moment she was definitely inclined to consider his regressions as fact rather than a psychological impairment of his brain.

Putting Michael Devilles' notes together had proved to be a rather daunting task, so Suzanne decided to once again, talk it over with her friends, Gerry and Meg at St Patrick's. So she telephoned and spoke to Meg, who suggested they also included Roland from the university. She volunteered, with a giggle, to contact 'Roly Poly' to stay at the Rectory the following weekend. Suzanne would also join them there and as Meg's two girls were to stay with friends, the Rectory would be entirely free to spend time reading through Suzanne's compilation of Michael's notes and recordings. They could then discuss and try to plan what should be done next.

~

Roland suggested that Suzanne talk to the owner of the magazine for which she worked to try and get him to publish the story in episodes, prior to the actual publication of a book. She thought this was a good idea.

The only item Suzanne had not researched in any detail was the Convent of the Golden Orb, which had little to offer through the internet. Therefore, it was agreed that the next step should be for her to visit Billenbach and discover what was to be learnt there.

It had been a successful and thoroughly pleasant weekend and the four friends arranged to meet again after Suzanne's visit to Switzerland.

Epilogue

Suzanne next spoke to Boris Slovinski, a rather taciturn man of Polish extraction. He had personally employed Suzanne when he first opened his offices in London. He had built up his magazine *International Viewpoint* over a period of fifteen years, ten of which had been from the city of London, and Suzanne had proved his expectations of her as an international investigative reporter many times over. Boris knew, in fact, that without his number one reporter the magazine would still be a small fish in a large pond; instead, he was swimming with the best and biggest of them, a successful and rich man.

In Boris's opinion, after reading Suzanne's transcription of the notes and discussing the matter with her it was obvious to him that there was only one thing to be done. The notes, as transcribed by Suzanne, were serialised in the magazine over a period of five weeks, under the title of, *The de Ville Papers*. The final episode appeared just two weeks prior to the publication of her book, entitled *Dark Regressions*.

With all the considerable previous publicity, the book was an immediate success, and Suzanne travelled from Lands' End to John o' Groats, signing copies.

Suzanne returned to the London office with an aching hand after an exhausting four weeks, only to be informed by Boris that he had made arrangements for her to make a similar trip throughout America. The book was due to be published in the USA in three months' time and meanwhile, he insisted that she take a holiday of at least one month. In fact, he presented her with first-class air tickets and information about the hotel reservation he had made for her in Switzerland.

"Switzerland Boris? And right in the mountains too, I notice? Isn't that the area where the Convent of the Golden Orb is?"

"Was my dear. The convent was closed down but not demolished. It was, in fact, bought from the estate of Henri de Ville's Count in 1953 and turned into an hotel."

"Ah! Hotel Orb de l'Or I presume?"

"You have it on the ball, as usual, Suzanne. I am only surprised you have not already investigated its whereabouts and poked around the history of the neighbourhood."

Suzanne frowned, knowing she had not followed her usual procedure when dealing with Michael's notes. Although she had followed up on information connected to Dr Jennings, Peter de Ville and James Cameron, she had not bothered to check out the Convent of the Golden Orb but just accepted all he had written as the facts as he had experienced them. They had discussed this at her meeting at the Rectory of St Patrick's and had already decided Switzerland should be high on her list of priorities. She had broken her number one rule before setting it down for publication. She had not checked the information before her, had not researched the Golden Orb angle.

"It's already on my to-do list, even if it is a bit late for that now," she said ruefully.

"Don't worry about it, I made sure the basic checks were made, don't want the magazine to hit a rock, do we? However, my dear, it might be interesting to poke around the old convent a bit. See if the caves are still there. The farmer family – what was their name?"

"Gelberger."

"Ah! That's right, Gelberger, is the family still there? If not, why not? You know my dear, etc…"

~

A week later, Suzanne was sitting on a bench in the sunny grounds of Hotel Orb de l'Or. She had arrived only the previous evening and been shown to a superbly appointed room overlooking the grounds towards the entrance gates. These were not closed nowadays but a security guard still occupied a small cottage just inside them. She decided to take a walk to the village after lunch. It would have grown since the time Lady Isabella de Ville was there but perhaps relatives of those who had lived in the area at that time would have their own stories of the past to relate.

The security guard was not in sight when Suzanne exited the gates, she would look out for him when she returned. Anyway, she had a full month when the conversation with that individual could be achieved. She thought the journey back to the hotel being a steep climb up the mountain path, would be harder to accomplish than the outward one.

Later, sitting at a table outside a small café with a mug of creamy chocolate before her, Suzanne felt the air cool as a shadow passed over her. She turned. Beside her stood a tall man, clad entirely in black with the exception of a crimson cravat at his neck. She shivered and instinctively glanced away from him. This was a man she knew. Not personally, but through the papers she had recently transcribed into a book and knew that to look into his eyes would be dangerous.

"May I join you?" The mellifluous voice rolled over her like a warm blanket on a cold day. "We have much to discuss, Lady."

Suzanne knew better than to issue an invitation of any description to this character. It was with a deep feeling of satisfaction that she realised at least she had learnt something of importance whilst carrying out her promise to Michael. Together with a sure knowledge that she must under no circumstances allow him to achieve eye contact with her,

"NO!"

Suzanne raised her voice and people at other tables looked toward her table. She rose and hurried into the teashop. When she looked out of the window, the man in black had gone, but she knew without a doubt that he would be back for her…